MW01254751

Raised as a Goon 4

Lock Down Publications and Ca$h
Presents

Raised as a Goon 4

A Novel by *Ghost*

Lock Down Publications
P.O. Box 870494
Mesquite, Tx 75187

Copyright 2018 by Ghost Raised as a Goon 4

All rights reserved. No part of this book may be reproduced in any form or by electronic or mechanical means, including information storage and retrieval systems without permission in writing from the publisher, except by a reviewer who may quote brief passages in review.
First Edition March 2018
Printed in the United States of America

This is a work of fiction. Names, characters, places, and incidents either are products of the author's imagination or are used fictitiously. Any similarity to actual events or locales or persons, living or dead, is entirely coincidental.

Lock Down Publications
Like our page on Facebook: Lock Down Publications @
www.facebook.com/lockdownpublications.ldp
Cover design and layout by: **Dynasty Cover Me**
Book interior design by: **Shawn Walker**

Stay Connected with Us!

Text **LOCKDOWN** to 22828 to stay up-to-date with new releases, sneak peaks, contests and more…

Thank you!

Submission Guideline.

Submit the first three chapters of your completed manuscript to ldpsubmissions@gmail.com, subject line: Your book's title. The manuscript must be in a .doc file and sent as an attachment. Document should be in Times New Roman, double spaced and in size 12 font. Also, provide your synopsis and full contact information. If sending multiple submissions, they must each be in a separate email.

Have a story but no way to send it electronically? You can still submit to LDP/Ca$h Presents. Send in the first three chapters, written or typed, of your completed manuscript to:

LDP: Submissions Dept
Po Box 870494
Mesquite, Tx 75187

DO NOT send original manuscript. Must be a duplicate.

Provide your synopsis and a cover letter containing your full contact information.

Thanks for considering LDP and Ca$h Presents.

Chapter 1
6 months later

I laid back on the bed and watched Princess stand in front of the full-length mirror, looking herself over closely as she stood in front of it wearing a Donatella Versace pink and black negligee that showed off her beautiful, brown round ass cheeks. She turned around to face me, then looked back over her shoulder and down at her ass in the mirror, biting on her juicy bottom lip, smiling.

"Damn, daddy, I don't know what you doin' to me, but whatever it is, you got me lookin' strapped. Baby girl thicka den a snicka. I *know* you see all this ass back here." she giggled, cuffing her cheeks and popping back on her legs.

I peeled off my polo shirt, leaving on my black wife beater and laid back, admiring my baby mother's lil' frame. She was definitely starting to get a lil' thick. Every time I get behind that ass, I make it my business to wear her ass out. She makes shit so easy and effortless being that she's extremely highly sexual.

"Yeah, boo, I see you lookin' a lil' pregnant back there. My baby girl gettin' thick." I agreed, nodding my head. Daddy, like that shit."

She turned around to face me, looking me in the eye. She sauntered over to me, bent at the waist and planted a soft kiss on my lips, wrapping her lil' arms around my neck, moaning into my mouth.

"Mhmm, I love you so much, daddy. I hope you know that. Long as you love how my body look, that's all that matters to me." She sucked on my lips with a bit more force, then put her face into the crook of my neck, biting me.

Damn, this girl! She knows that shit always turns me on and make me wanna murder her lil' ass.

I grabbed her by the waist and lifted her onto me, laying straight back so that she was positioned on top of me perfectly.

She placed both of her knees on each side of my body. I reached around and firmly gripped that *new* booty, rubbing all over it, slightly pulling her cheeks apart, so she could feel that air hit her ass hole.

As I rose up a lil' bit, I could see our reflection in the full-length mirror. I was mesmerized by the way the negligee rose up to her waist, fully exposing her sex lips from the back. Watching the way my big hands played all over her ass, drove a nigga crazy.

She was so little in comparison to me, but it never stopped her from taking that dick like a champion.

My fingers had a mind of their own as they made their way to her opening, her wetness inviting them in, first one, then two. She let out a soft moan deep within her throat as she threw her head back. My fingers stretched her, causing her to arch her back and purr out her transgressions.

"Mhmm, Daddy. You want some of yo baby girl, don't you? Mmm, I know you do." She groaned, biting into my neck a little harder.

The bathroom door to our room opened wide, and Blaze appeared from behind it. "Dang, y'all ain't even gon' wait for me?" She questioned in a whiny tone, making her way over to the bed in one of our big Burberry drying towels.

She stood in front of us, allowing the towel to release its hold from her body as she made eye contact with me.

My eyes trailed up and down her thick ass body, as she caressed herself, squeezin' her titties together and pulling on her erect nipples. She slid her hand down her stomach, spread her thighs and separated her pussy lips while she watched Princess continue to suck all over my neck, moaning and my fingers persistent with the assault they inflicted on her pussy. In and out they went, at a rapid pace. Her breathing labored and body jerking as her juices dripped onto my stomach, a small pool of it forming inside of my navel.

"Mmmm. Daddy make her come. Over here. Make her eat me from the back. She do that shit so well. I love that shit. Please, daddy." Princess begged, sliding her hand in between us and gripping my dick hard.

I spread my knees, which forced Princess to open her thighs wider. From the reflection in the mirror, her pussy was bussed all the way open. My fingers were drenched in her fluids.

"You heard her." I ordered, looking over at Blaze. "Get yo ass over here and eat my baby girl. Hurry up, ma. Then its yo turn. You hear me?" Princess pulled my dick fully out of my boxers.

She slid down my body with her ass in the air, still facing me, gripped my dick and stroked it up and down as it rested against her cheek, all the while looking over her shoulder at Blaze.

"C'mon, Blaze. Make me cum before my daddy fuck me. Besides him, don't nobody eat me like you do."

Blaze allowed her two fingers to slide into her own hot box, running them in and out of herself before pulling them out and sampling her juices. She squatted down behind Princess, pushing her forward so that her face was buried into my chest.

"I'ma eat this pussy, Taurus, but after that you gotta fuck me until my shit hurt. I need you to put that gangsta dick on me like you always do when I come to town. Can you promise me that?" she asked, looking over the small of Princess' back.

Princess popped her head, looking slightly annoyed. "Once again, you gettin' shit twisted, Blaze. Taurus is gon' fuck you only if I say he can. I thought we already had that fact understood." She frowned her face, raising her right eyebrow.

Blaze started to bite on her finger nail. "I understand that, Princess, it's just that I wanted to make sure. I ain't seen y'all in a while and since I been back, Taurus ain't been givin' me no play like that. I know you got his ass locked down, so I can't be too sure." She placed both of her hands on Princess' ass, spreading her cheeks apart. "I don't mind pleasin' you. You always taste good to me." She stuffed her face between Princess' ass cheeks, changing her tone. All I could hear were the slurping sounds of Blaze putting that work in, occupying the room.

"Un. Un. Un. Ummm. Shit. Blaze. I swear to. Ummm. Dis bitch." Princess moaned inaudibly, sucking all over my chest while she continued to stroke my piece. She raised up some more, pushing her ass back into Blaze's face, allowing her more access.

She welcomed my dick into her mouth, deep throating me inch by inch, with no hands. When she came to the top of my dick, she'd rub her face all around it, then she'd suck him back into her mouth like a vacuum.

Over time, she had perfected her gag reflex. I was impressed and speechless at the same time, with my eyes rolling into the back of my head and biting into my bottom lip. The feeling was indescribable.

"Hmmm," I groaned, trying my best not to cum too soon. But with the combination of sounds coming from

Blaze and Princess, and Princess performing on me like a porn star, all at once, was enough to drive a nigga crazy.

I was anxious to see them fuck each other, especially when they assumed the 69 position. It was the norm whenever Blaze came to town but being that it had been over a month since Princess and I's last encounter with her, I think I was more excited. They had always put on a show for me which ended with me wearing both of their asses out.

Princess popped my dick out of her mouth and threw her head back, which I knew meant that she was on the verge of cumming. "Un. Un. Un. Awww, shit. I'm cumming! Blaze! Awww, shit! Pleeasseeeee. Don't stop. While I cum all in yo pretty ass mouth!" she screamed, as she leaned forward, opening her ass cheeks as far as they would go while she shook on top of me. "Unnnnnn!"

After Blaze knew that she'd cum, she stood up and squeezed her titties together, her nipples super hard. There was pussy juice all over her thick lips that caused them to shine in the dim room.

"Okay, I held up my end, now I want some of you, Taurus. Please come fuck me." She bit into her bottom lip, looking me in the eyes, all sexy like.

The way she stared at me made my dick jump. Princess mean mugged me, so I knew she felt that. She climbed off me and sat on the side of me. "A'ight. I see what this is, Taurus, you wanna fuck that bitch just as bad as she wanna fuck you, huh?" she snapped, grabbing my dick and squeezing it roughly as it stood at attention with the head pointing past my navel, throbbing like crazy. If she was looking for an honest response, there it was.

"Hell yeah!" I exclaimed. "I want some of that shit. I ain't had it in a while." I could barely talk because my breathing was so labored. Blaze was perfectly shaped, and her body was that of a top-notch, money-making stripper. That's how she made her money all around the United States.

She could go to any club in the U.S. and be the head liner, charging them a fee just to step out on to their stage. She was able to keep 90 percent of her intake, and that wasn't including her fee for just showing up. Then on top of that, her pussy always fit me like a glove.

I couldn't comprehend how wonderfully crafted her body was and how her pussy was so tight and unmistakably wet on in the inside. That shit drove me nuts.

Blaze stepped closer to the bed and placed a knee on to it, ready to climb aboard, not once taking her eyes off mine. I looked past her and into the full-length mirror that was on the back of our bedroom door and caught the view of her ass from that angle. Her pussy mimicked that of an angry blowfish.

"Please, Princess. Please, let me have some of him now. I'm feenin' for him." She started to shiver, crawling to me on her knees across the king-sized bed.

Princess jumped out of the bed, stomped around and grabbed a handful of Blaze's hair, yanking her head back violently.

"Bitch, you love my nigga's dick, huh?" she grunted, mugging her.

Blaze nodded her head, still never taking her eyes off me. "Please, Princess. I ain't tryna to step on yo toes, just let him fuck me, then I'll leave y'all crib right after. I need some bad. These other niggaz don't fuck me like he do," she begged.

Princess yanked her by the hair even harder, causing her to wince out in pain. For the first time, she took her eyes off me and closed them.

"Bitch, this my nigga. You gotta go find you a nigga that get down like him 'cuz I run that pipe between his legs. You got that?" she asked through clenched teeth.

I wanted to get up and break that shit up but when it came to Princess, her temper was just as horrible as mine.

Even though I liked fucking Blaze, it wasn't worth beefing with my baby mother. We'd been through way too much together, and we was in this shit until the death.

Blaze blinked, allowing a single tear to roll down her cheek. "Okay, I'll go. Just let me put my clothes on." Princess let her go.

As soon as she did, Blaze jumped up, slid into her Prada dress and slid up her Victoria Secret's Pink collection purple boy short laced panties before grabbing her Michael Kors jacket out of the closet, sliding her arms into the sleeves.

I felt sick as hell for how Princess had treated her. I wanted to get up and console her. At least walk her out to her Bentley, but I knew better. If ever me and Blaze got down, we'd have to be on some creeping shit because it didn't seem like Princess was going for it anymore.

And the way I was, I knew I wouldn't cross my baby girl like that, even though Blaze's pussy was so fire.

We watched her get fully dressed, sliding her last foot into her red bottom three-inch heels. She looked over her shoulder at me. "I guess I'll see you later, Taurus." She opened the bedroom door and stepped out into the hallway.

Princess turned to me and smiled. "A'ight, daddy, now go snatch that bitch up and take her pussy. I mean fuck her like a savage. You already know what that bitch need and we gotta keep her money flowing in this direction." She curled her upper lip and I knew that she was thinking how I was thinking.

I jumped out of that bed, and into the hallway just as Blaze was opening the front door to our house. "Where the fuck you think you going?" I asked with

a scowl on my face.

She bucked her eyes. "I'm just gon' go fuck with Screw and nem' until I fly back out to Miami in the morning. I wish…"

I ran up on her and put my hand around her neck, squeezing, before biting into it roughly and pulling her dress up at the same time. Then I picked her up into the air, smashing her back against the door.

"Uh! Shit! Taurus! What are you doing?" She moaned, as I reached between us, hooked a finger into the leg hole of her boy shorts, ripping it enough to expose her bald, sex lips.

Bitch, you think you finna leave my crib without me hitting this pussy? Huh? You don't run shit, Blaze. I keep on telling you that." I angled my dick the right way and put the head on her hole, slamming her down on it with force. "Uhhhh! Fuck Taurus! Fuck! You in me again! Awww! Shit! Yes!"

she screamed, as I got to bouncing her up and down on my pipe. Her heat searing my pole and gripping it at the same time.

"Un. Un. Un. Un. Oh. Oh. Awww. Shit. Yes. Yes. Fuck me. Taurus. Fuck me. Hurt me. Hurt me. Please. Yes! Yes! Yessss!" she hollered. "I'm cumming! I'm cumming already! Uhhh!"

I really got to bouncing her up and down then while she creamed all over me, then I fell to the floor with her and ripped her dress down the middle, exposing her perky brown titties with the big chocolate nipples. I reached down and ripped her panties all the way from her frame, causing her ass to rise from the white carpet again and again until I got them free.

Once free I pushed her knees to her chest, I slid back in and got to fucking her with all my might. “This my pussy, Blaze! This my shit! You hear me? Huh? Tell me!” I hollered, slamming that cat with force.

Bam! Bam! Bam!

Digging deep into her center while she lay in a ball pinned under me.

“Awww, shit! Aw, shit! You killing me! Aww, Taurus! You fucking. You fucking. You fucking me! You fucking me too hard. I can’t take it. I can’t! Uhhhh, shit! I’m cuming! I’m cuming! Uhhh mmmyyyy Goddd-a!” She hollered, her pussy squirting juices at me as if she were peeing.

I flipped her ass over on to her stomach, then I pulled her up by her hips. There was no way that I was about to let her fly back to Miami without me hitting that shit from the back. She was too thick. And the way I saw it, if a woman was as strapped as she was, one was supposed to have that pussy beat in from the back by a goon like me.

I grabbed a hand full of her hair and forced her face into the carpet, then I got to long stroking that shit while my abs slammed into her thick ass cheeks, causing them to jiggle and shake.

Blaze was screaming in ecstasy. “Ummm! Ummm! Ummm! Yes, Taurus! This yo pussy. Don’t nobody fuck me! Uhhh, like you do!” She cried with tears running down her cheeks.

Princess came into the living room and crawled under her, forcing Blaze to put her face in her lap while she held her pussy lips open for her. “Eat me some more, Blaze, while my daddy fuck you until you can’t sit no more.”

After she said this, I looked down at her and noted she had a bottle of KY that we used when I fucked her in the back doe. She held it up, before tossing it to me.

"All that ass she got back there, daddy, I know you wanna hit that shit and I don't blame you. I wish I had a dick so I could hit that shit, too. Fuck that big booty, daddy. Make her feel that shit." Princess grabbed a handful of her hair and made her lift her face up. "You want him to fuck that ass, bitch? Huh? Keep that shit real?" Princess hollered, grabbing Blaze's tit and squeezing it.

I didn't even hear Blaze's answer. I had already slid out of her pussy, squirted some of that oil into my hands and jagged my dick with it before sliding slowly into her ass and forcing her face back into Princess' crotch, then I got to rocking that muhfucka on my G-shit, loving the way it rippled. I grabbed her hips and forced her to slam back into me, while she hollered and cried real tears. Princess played with her clitoris, pinching it between her fingers. "Unn. Unn. Unn. I love y'all! Uhh! Shit. I love y'all, Taurus. I swear to God I do!"

I got to fucking her with all my might in that big booty, until she came, and then I pulled out and came all over her ass while Princess rubbed it into her thick ass cheeks.

About two hours later, after we all showered, I walked her out to her Bentley with my right arm around her, kissing on her cheek every few steps. "You know you my baby, right?" I asked, smelling her Prada perfume wharf up my nose.

To me there was nothing like a woman that smelled good and stayed on top of their fashion game. Women that took care of themselves made men like me want to spend a bag on them with no remorse. Blaze was the type of sista that always stayed tip top. Her swag alone was one of the reasons why I could never just release her. Her pussy kept on calling me back, too. I loved being in her presence.

She turned to look up at me. "Taurus, I meant what I said back there. I mean not about Princess but about you. I really do love you and one of these days, I'm gon' take you away from her because you belong with me. Don't nobody do me like you do. I hate these other niggaz because they ain't got yo swag. They ain't official. I been all around the world, and you are the last of a dying breed." She popped her doors using her remote on her keys. The pink Bentley's Ferrari's driver door slowly opened upward before she walked around to it. She stopped and stood on her tippy toes, kissing me on the lips. "I wanna tell you something, but I don't want you to freak out and I need for you to know that I would never lie to you. I'm more of a woman than that." She reached up and held the side of my face, as the sun beamed down on us, causing the July summer to feel that much hotter. It was so humid I could barely breathe out there. My Secret deodorant was turning moist under my arms.

"A'ight now! Y'all looking way too lovey dovey out there for me! Taurus get yo ass in the house before I come out there and shoot you and Blaze! Hurry up!" Princess yelled, then she slammed the door to our crib so hard I wondered if she was actually going to get one of our many pistols.

Blaze held my face in her hands. "Taurus, I'm pregnant by you. I know it's your child because for the last year I haven't slept with any man besides you. Now I'm not asking you for anything. Financially, I can handle my own business. Our child will have the best of the best. The one thing I do ask of you is that you have a presence in our lives. I love you, and I honestly want to be with just you. I got three club dates booked, then I'm done for a while." She took a deep breath, then looked back up to me exhaling slowly.

My head was spinning, and I felt like I was about to pass out. I didn't really know what to say in that moment because I was so caught off guard. I mean, I cared about Blaze and I knew we were fucking without protection, which was dangerous within itself. I just didn't factor in the whole baby chances, but I would stand up and handle my business as a man, that was without a doubt. I was just worried because Princess was finna go ballistic. She might even try to kill Blaze.

"Look, Blaze, I care about you like a muhfucka. You're in my heart second to my baby mother. I'm down for you in any way that you need me to be. That's my word." I wrapped her into my arms and hugged her lovingly.

She hugged me back. "Baby, I ain't trying to cause you no discomfort, I just wanted to let you know what it was. This is your child and for the rest of my life, I'm going to be your woman. I told you that I was going to help you become a boss, right?" she asked, looking up at me.

I nodded. "You did, and you put me in with the right niggaz out here. I'll never forget that."

"Just always know that I ride for you, Taurus, and that Princess isn't all that you have."

After she said that, Princess came out of the house with a gun in her hand, cocking it back. "Y'all think I'm playin', huh?"

"I love you, Taurus." Blaze jumped into her Bentley, started it up and pulled out of our driveway with her driver's door still up.

Chapter 2

The next day, I found myself sitting across from Hood Rich at his mansion out in Dallas, while he placed a bundle of cash beside him and started to fill it into the money counting machine.

The machine made a loud noise as it counted the bills before it gave Hood Rich its total digitally on the side of it.

"Taurus, we gotta track down that nigga, Meech, real soon because he causing a whole lot of problems for my organization. I'm hearing that he been sending his lil' hittas into my blow houses back in Chicago and stripping them down. Four of my safe houses also got hit in the last three months, and we were supposed to handle some business out in Boston for one of the Mafia bosses by the name of Don Bertolli. Instead of Meech waiting for me, he went ahead and took care of things with this make shift crew that he assembled, and they fucked shit up real bad. Some of the wrong men got killed and the Don calling for me to right this wrong because he'd previously set the mission in front of me and not Meech. If that ain't enough, do you remember Nastia?" he asked, feeding the machine another bundle of cash.

It flickered loudly as it counted the bundle that wound up on the other side of it in a neat stack. The digital screen read twelve thousand and I noted there was a big ass pile that he had not even counted yet.

He pushed about a quarter of the money across the table at me and pointed to the machine that I was sitting in front of that was identical to the one he was using. "Taurus, count that shit for me, lil' bruh?"

I nodded and flipped the switch on my machine. I picked up a bundle of cash and set it into the feeder. "Yeah,

I remember Nastia, bruh. What's good with her?" I asked, as my machine sucked in the money.

Hood Rich lowered his head. "Nastia missing and I got a feeling that nigga, Meech, got something to do with it. You know they used to fuck around for a minute back in the day. Nastia don't really fuck with her own people. She know that most of them is racist bastards and back in her home land, they treat the women like shit. Long story short, she got her old man wrapped around her finger. And back in Russia, instead of him trusting most of their family business to her bro that got killed down in Memphis, he was leaning on her, not knowing that she was soaking up the game and bussing moves on her own. She helped me and Meech with this rebirth shit. Helped us flood the states and in less than five years, we weren't seeing no less than a million a day. And that's after we fed everybody that needed to be fed and reinvested into our products across the states. Anyway, once her old man found out, he ain't like that shit and he started to send a lot of heat our way. He had Russians blowing up our whips, shooting up our cribs and murdering the niggaz that worked for us across the country. About a month ago, while I was over in London fucking off with this lil' model bitch, he called himself sending a few of his hittas at me with the message that his daughter was missing and that I needed to find her or prepare myself for an all-out war. Now this ain't the type of war that niggaz used to in the hood. Nall, when I say war, I mean on my money and on my businesses across the world. Then there is also the murdering factor." He picked up a bundle of money and placed it in his big safe that was on wheels beside him. It looked like a refrigerator.

I placed a bundle of cash to the side, then I slid it across the table to him. "This thirteen thousand right here." He grabbed it and placed it inside of his safe with the rest of his cash before continuing the process of counting another pile. "Hood Rich, what I don't understand is why would that fool Meech cross you in the first place. You dudes are legends back in the Land."

Hood Rich placed another bundle into his safe and shook his head, exhaling loudly. "Meech fuckin' with The Rebirth and it's causing him to make some stupid ass decisions that's gon' get his life took." He curled his upper lip. "I don't take kindly to no nigga breaking they bond of loyalty with me, especially once you swear that shit in blood, homie. That's as serious as it gets. I mean, you from Chicago. You know how that shit go back home. Niggaz will take the life of every member of yo family for some shit like that. Now, I grew up with that nigga. Ate off the floor with that nigga. Our mothers bathed us in the same sink, at the same, time when we were shorties and this how that fool repaid me?" He frowned and reloaded the money machine.

He continued to shake his head as if he were in deep thought.

I really didn't know what to say, so I kept on feeding my machine and placed the counted money to the side after writing down the total.

As we were working, two bad ass Brazilian looking broads stepped into the room with long curly hair, thick as a peanut butter sandwich, and only dressed in see-through red laced bras and red G string panties.

One of them stepped up to me and I looked on the gold tray and saw that it was our lunch. A well-done Porter house steak, baked potato and a portion of broccoli with melted cheese on top of it. A bottle of strawberry Moet and a rolled blunt of some Tropical Loud.

I mean, I couldn't see inside of the Cuban Cigar, but I knew how Hood Rich got down. The pretty thang looked down on me and smiled, two dimples popping up on her cheeks.

"Are you hungry, baby? If so, can I cut up your steak and feed it to you?" She licked her lips, then she bit into her bottom one.

I trailed my eyes up and down her body, hungrily. This bitch was bad enough for me to get in trouble with Princess.

Hood Rich shook his head, then he waved them off. "Nall, not right now. I'm lacing my lil' nigga in this moment. Y'all take that shit back upstairs and I'll let you know when to reheat it. I know when I get up there that my mansion better be cleaned from top to bottom. I shouldn't smell shit but Febreze and the scent of you hoez' perfumes. Y'all getting me right now?" he asked, looking heated.

They both nodded in unison, took the gold trays of food and made their way back out of the den with me looking at their fat asses. I didn't know what it was about Brazilian broads, but it seemed like they were the only females that could stand next to our sistas in the ass department. Now don't get me wrong, they definitely weren't on they level, but they were somewhere in second place, a distant second.

After they left, Hood Rich got up and closed the door. "The bottom line is that we about to be at war with Meech. I'm taking you back to the Land with me, and we gon' tear that muhfucka up until we find this nigga. You gotta get yo hands dirty, Taurus, but I'm gon' make it all worth yo while. You fuck with me and we handle this bitness with this nigga and find Nastia, bruh, I'll make you beyond a rich man. A fucking legend. Clover City is already gon' be yours. While we handling this bitness, we gon' set that shit in motion, too. Fuck with Screw and Flip out that way to get them slums in order." he stepped over to me and looked down into my face. "I need you to stand up, lil' homie, and look me in my eyes."

I set the bundle of cash that I had in my hand down on the table and stood up, damn near forehead to forehead with Hood Rich. I didn't know what the homie had on his mind, but I really didn't like being that close in proximity to no man. I mean, bruh was cool but still I felt kind of awkward.

"What's good, Hood Rich?" I asked, taking just a minor step back.

He curled his upper lip and frowned his face. "I need to know if you gon' hold me down, Taurus? I don't really trust no niggaz out here in this world. But seeing as I helped you get back your mother and your daughter, I feel we good. Plus, I murked a bunch of them blood niggaz before I even got down with you like that just to let you know that I'm a real nigga. I feel like I should be able to trust you. Ain't nothin' thicker than the blood around you, homie." He looked me up and down and sucked his teeth.

I didn't know what all them theatrics was about, but I did feel like I owed the homie my loyalty.

Six months ago, he'd saved my daughter and my mother. Then on top of that, he helped me bring my brother to justice. My turn coat ass brother, Juice, that had raped my mother multiple times, kidnapped my daughter and bodied my sister, my right-hand man and my baby mother's brother, who in fact was supposed to be his right-hand man at the time.

Juice had taken me and my family through so much. I tore up the whole Memphis trying to find his ass and couldn't. The only one that was able to do that before he killed my daughter and mother was Hood Rich. So, yeah, I owed him my loyalty in blood.

"Look, Hood Rich, what you did for me I can never repay you back for, but what I can do is ride with you til' the dirt. I don't know everything that Meech did to you but since he crossed you, my nigga, then that means that he crossed me, too. I pledge my loyalty to you in blood. Right now, and until we handle this bitness. Far as Nastia go, if anybody can find her, it's me. So, just let me know what I gotta do, and it's done. I mean that shit."

Hood Rich didn't say a word for what seemed like a full minute. Just continued to look me in the eyes. "You know what, Taurus? I don't know what it is about you, lil' homie, but I believe you and keep in mind that I don't trust in or believe in no nigga. But it's something about you that I feel in my heart I can trust yo loyalty." He extended his hand and I shook it before he gave me a half hug. "Nigga, this shit ain't finna be easy. We about to go up against some giants in the game. I need to know that you can handle this shit because the game is unforgiving. Long as you got my back I got yours. Just know that once we buss, it all falls down. Take you a few days to get yo mind right. We fly out to Chicago this Saturday in search of that nigga Meech. Is there anything that you need before then?" he asked, releasing me and sitting down at the table of money.

"The only thing I need to make sure of is that Princess, my mother and my daughter gon' be safe throughout all of this." I shook my head. "Oh, and Blaze. She holding my seed right now, so that means that I gotta protect her at all costs."

Hood Rich exhaled and shook his head. "I can't lie to you, bruh. Once we bomb first, everybody is in jeopardy, including our families. Shid, to be honest with you, they in jeopardy right now. This shit is bigger than the hood or any of that shit that you used to. You fuckin' with power players in the game that got millions to blow on some war shit. At every turn, something could be waiting on yo ass. In the last three months, I done had four whips blow up. This shit is real. So, while I can't promise you that yo people won't be targeted, what I can do is put a million dollars' worth of protection for them. Consider that done."

Back at my house, Princess paced back and forth, shaking her head from side to side, while Jahliya ate a peanut butter and jelly sandwich at the table, singing a song to herself. "I juss wanna Rollie, Rollie, Rollie and a diamond wing." She sang with her mouth full of food.

It took everything in me to not crack up because Princess was pacing back and forth in front of me with a mug on her face.

"Baby, what's the matter?" I asked trying to grab her arm, but she yanked it away from me in anger.

"Taurus, word is bond leave me alone right now while I'm trying to think. This shit you just told me is fucking me up, both of 'em." She frowned her face even harder and shook her head. "How this bitch know it's yo kid, though? She a muhfucking stripper.

I mean, don't them hoez get around?" she asked, talking more to herself than me. "Then why the fuck Hood Rich gotta take you with him. This nigga got all the money in the world. He can pay niggaz to do everything he finna have you do. I don't like this shit because you got a whole ass family over here that need you. You can't be playin' in them streets like that no mo, Taurus. Word is bond, if you wind up getting kilt, I'ma revive you then kill yo ass again. What the fuck am I gon' do if you ain't on this earth? You know I need you like crazy and so does Jahliya. Fuck!" She hollered and started to walk faster back and forth in front of me.

She hollered so loud that Jahliya wound up knocking over her glass of milk. It spilled onto the table before dripping to the floor. As soon as it happened, Jahliya's eyes got bucked, then she looked into the dining room toward Princess and started to cry.

"I'm sorry, Mommy. I'm sorry." She got out of the chair and tried to clean it up before I stepped into the kitchen to help her.

"It's okay, baby. Daddy know you didn't do it on purpose. I got it. Just give me kiss," I said, placing her dishes into the sink.

I came back over and picked her up, puckering my lips before she kissed me and wrapped her little arms around my neck. "Thank you, baby, now go play in your room." I put her down and watched her run off into the back of the house.

Princess stepped into the kitchen. "Taurus, tell that bitch to get an abortion. I don't want nobody else having yo kids. I'm the only baby mother you're supposed to have. We been through too much together. Word is bond, just me knowing that she pregnant it's making me wanna kill her ass and I can't control these urges." She looked at the floor. "Then as far as you going with Hood Rich, how long is y'all supposed to be gone for? He ain't talking no months or nothin' is he?" She asked, looking up at me with a worried expression on her face.

I sighed. "Princess, you working yo self up way too much. I'm thinking we might be gon' for a few days. I'll keep checking in with you to keep you updated. Far as Blaze go, that shit ain't happening. I'll never kill one of my kids. You wylin' on even bringing some shit like that up." I mugged the shit out of her.

Then I started to wash the dishes in the sink because them being there was driving me crazy. I was a real neat freak when it came to my crib. Everything had to be tidy and fresh. Even though Princess did a decent job at cleaning, I always went behind her and did my own thing.

Princess put her hand on my shoulder and turned me around, so I could face her. "So, you gon' let this bitch have yo kid, then? What? I'm supposed to accept her as being a part of our lives? She equal to me now because she giving you a baby?" She looked hurt. "Nall, fuck that. She already makes me insecure because that bitch got some type of hold on you that I can't explain but as a woman I just sense it. I ain't strong enough to endure that competition, Taurus. I feel like I'ma lose you to that pretty bitch and that's gon' make me go on a rampage." She sunk down to the floor on her butt, with tears streaming down her face. "Damn, I knew I should have nipped that shit in the bud. Now I gotta go through this shit. I just want you to myself. I thought we already had that understanding?"

I dried my hands, turned around and knelt beside her wrapping her into my arms. "Baby, I swear you over thinking shit way too much. Me and you are forever. I love you to death. I'd never choose nobody over you. Just because she's pregnant that doesn't mean that I'm finna switch up on my baby girl. How could I ever do that? Huh? After all me and you been through?" I kissed her soft cheek and kissed away her falling tears that tasted salty.

"I know, Taurus, but I just want you all to myself. I don't want to share you with nobody, not even our daughter, really. And I know that sounds selfish so to say, but I never had a man in this world really care about me the way that you do. For the first time in my life, I really understand what love really means, and it's all because of you. You're the best daddy that I could ever ask for. Now I gotta share you with this bitch until her child turn eighteen. I swear, I think I might kill her, Taurus. I swear, I'm serious. You know how I am. You know I would never lie to you. But I can't compete with her. She makes me feel so ugly, even when you tell me I'm beautiful. I see the way you look at her body and it makes me feel so insecure because my body would never look like hers. I'm gon' be slim for the rest of my life and I know you really want some thin thick like her. Its killing me!" She hollered and broke into a fit of tears.

I hugged her tighter. "You buggin', ma. You are the perfect woman for me in every single way. Our love surpasses that physical shit that you sittin' here stressing about. I love you way too much for you to break down on me right now. You're my everything. Never forget that." I pulled her into my embrace and held her while she cried, until she came out of her depressive state of mind about two hours later.

After it was all said and done she calmed down enough to catch her breath, she looked up at me. "Daddy, you know I'd never lie to you about anything because for as long as we've been together, we've always been up front with one another." She exhaled loudly and shook her head slowly. "Well, I'm gon' let you know that on a scale of one to ten, with ten being me actually doin' it, I'm at a nine for seeing myself killing Blaze. I don't want that bitch on this earth, if she got your kid. So, I'm telling you right now that if one morning you wake up in our bed and I ain't beside you, it's because I'm out there looking to find this bitch, and ain't nothin' you gon' say that will stop me." After saying that, she stood up and walked to the back of the house where our room was. "Ain't no bitch having yo kid with me alive,

Taurus. No bitch!" She slammed the door and all I could do was lower my head as I heard Jahliya crying.

Chapter 3

The next day, at about three in the morning, I found myself loading on to Hood Rich's private jet with four heavily armed body guards climbing on board behind me and him.

There were already two thick ass Puerto Rican's on the Jet dressed in real tight Gucci stewardess uniforms. Theirs tops were unbuttoned so low that I could make out most of their titties and nipples. Every time they walked back and forth, the little skirts would rise to show off the bottom haves of their asses.

I sat back in the red leather Louis Vuitton seats, as one of them handed me a bottle of Moet that was cool to the touch. I could tell that it had been kept in the refrigerator. Along with that, she gave me a freshly rolled Cuban cigar that was filled with Tropical Loud.

Hood rich sat down across from me and received the same treatment. He lit his blunt, so I lit mine and inhaled the weed smoke. It filled my lungs, taking over my mental right away. I popped the cork and handed it to the stewardess, then I watched her walk away with her skirt up so high I could see the Victoria Secret thong in her ass crack.

"When we get down here, Taurus, we ain't playing no games. It's a few niggaz that I used to fuck with back in the day that I heard still doing bitness with Meech, so they gon' know where he at. We just gotta get that shit out of 'em. Now, I don't know how long it's been since you been back home to Chicago but that muhfucka done changed. If you thought niggaz was cold hearted way back when, then you gon' be in for a rude awakening because now its fucked up. Everybody doing them pills and fuckin with The Rebirth, so the city is dying at a rapid pace. We gotta be on guard, and don't trust none of these niggaz. Hunh." He reached on the side of him and opened a little Louis Vuitton chest, reached into it and pulled out an all-black bullet proof vest that had FBI written across the front of it. When I took it, it felt real heavy. "Put this muhfucka on right now because it ain't no telling if the enemy knows I'm landing at O'Hare in a minute or not. You just can't be too safe." He shed his Gucci top, and put a vest on as well before throwing his shirt back on.

I put mine in place and tightened it so that it fit snug to my frame. "So, what's the purpose for us going down here? Is it just to find Meech or is it to handle some other unfinished bitness, as well? I can guess that a bunch of niggaz crossed you, so if you ready to pay they ass back, I'm just letting you know that I'm down for the cause, big homie." I took a strong pull from my blunt and chased it with the Moet, swallowing big gulps, feeling the bubbles tickle my throat.

Hood Rich curled his upper lip. "We finna fuck some shit up, Taurus. All these niggaz think that because I got money that I ain't still about that life. Like I won't get my hands dirty and wash them bitchez in they blood. I got my hittas with me, but that's just to watch our backs. All these niggaz that we about to hit up we gon' do on our own. Somebody finna tell me where Meech is!" He slammed his fist down on the table, shocking me a lil' bit because before that loud ass noise, the only sounds were of Twista spitting low versus throughout the speakers. So, that sudden noise made me jump and it irritated me. "We gotta find that nigga, Taurus, and then we gotta find that white bitch before them Russians be all over our ass. I ain't trying to be going to war with them just yet. That's gon' put a damper on our money."

I sat back in the soft leather seat after mugging him for a second, then I took another sip of the Moet. "Bruh, like I said, I'm down for whatever."

Two hours later, and just as the sun was starting to peak through the clouds, Hood Rich pulled his all-black Hummer up in front of a two-story, white bricked house that had two Benz parked in the driveway.

He turned off the ignition and threw some black leather gloves on my lap. "This nigga named Poppa. Me and Meech grew up with him and made this once bum ass nigga rich. If anybody knows where that fool hiding out, its him. Thing is, he one of them old heads that's stuck in his ways. Been living in the land of the heartless for so long, untouched, that he feels like he's invincible. We about to change all that shit. I don't give a fuck who in this crib, Taurus, everybody in jeopardy until we get a lead to Meech. You got that?"

I nodded my head as I finished fitting the gloves over my hands and pulling the white ski mask down over my face. Hood Rich put his arm out of the window of the Hummer and did some sort of signal. The next thing I knew, four dudes jumped out of the black Navigator that was trailing us around the city and ran across Poppa's lawn. Two stopped at the front door, and two went to the back of the house with their pistols in their hands.

I lowered myself in my seat and looked around the neighborhood. It looked like your average middle-class neighborhood. All the lawns were manicured, with nice cars in each of the driveways. I imagined that the police made frequent rounds. I got a lil' paranoid and hoped that Hood Rich knew what he was doing. The last thing I needed was to be locked up in the Illinois state pen. I was already on the run from Tennessee. I knew that both of those states traded prisoners back and forth like baseball cards.

Fuck that! Before I got lost to the system, I would hold court in the streets. I was serious about that and already knew that was how my chapter would end.

I looked back over to the house as the front door opened and one of Hood Rich's goons waved us over.

"Come on, lil' homie, let's make this nigga talk. I want you to watch me slice his ass up like you did Juice until he tells me what I wanna know," Hood Rich said, opening his driver's door.

I followed him across the lawn and into the house. The first thing I saw was that his goons had two females laid on their stomachs in the living room with duct tape on their mouths.

They looked like they were about fifteen or sixteen years old and had went to sleep with barely anything on. Their hands were also duct taped behind their backs and they were dressed in skimpy panties and bras. I figured they must have been Poppa's daughters. But then we made it into the dining room of the crib, we saw there were four more of them around the same age. These girls were completely naked, and duct taped.

Two of them looked to be black and the other two of Spanish descent. I was confused but continued to follow Hood Rich toward the back of the house, making our way through the kitchen where three other young girls were sat up against the wall, naked with duct tape over their mouths and hands. Every time they kicked their legs trying to free themselves, they exposed their jewels to us. I could hear them hollering into the tape, but I couldn't make out what they were saying.

We went up a flight of stair, down a hallway and then up a ladder that led into the attic. Once there, Hood Rich started to laugh, removing his mask. "Ha, ha, you bitch ass nigga. Look at you now. All tied up and shit. You and this rotten bitch."

I finished climbing the ladder and as soon as I got all the way up into the attic, I saw that a dark-skinned dude with a real long perm was duct taped to a chair by his hands and feet. He was naked with the exception of his boxers. A big gut sat in his lap. He looked to be about forty something years old. Beside him in another chair duct taped the same way was a real pretty older chick, yellow with freckles all over her face. She was ass naked and sitting there calmer than the squirming Poppa beside her.

Hood Rich walked up to Poppa and tore the duct tape away from his face. Before he could ask him a question, Poppa started runnin' his mouth.

"Look I already know why you here, Hood Rich, but that shit between you and Meech ain't got shit to do with me and my lady. We ain't fucking with the dope game no moe, it's all about under age pussy for us now. Sex trafficking. That's where them chips at. I'm retired from that old life, Boss." He rolled his head around on his neck, breathing all hard and shit.

Hood Rich laughed once again, then he reached and smacked him so hard that it split Poppa's lip and made him spit blood across the room.

Wham!

Poppa's head snapped to the side before Hood Rich grabbed him by the throat, slipped a knife out of the small of his back and slammed it into Poppa's thigh, twisting it.

"Awww! Awww! What the fuck? Hood Rich! Come on, man! I ain't did shit to you!"

Smack! Smack! Smack!

Hood Rich had his head going from side to side. "Where the fuck Meech at and who gave the order for niggaz to run in my trap houses?" He hollered with his forehead against Poppa's.

The knife remained in his thigh, with blood pooling around it before it dripped down his leg and on to his ankles before the floor.

Poppa's bottom lip quivered. His body shook. His eyes were watery, and I had to smile at that. Niggaz always turnt bitch when the heat was on. I never understood that shit. When my time came, I promised to go out like a man. I wasn't bowing down to no nigga and begging for my life. Fuck that. I could never look God in the eye if I did.

Poppa exhaled loudly and shook his head. "I don't know, Hood Rich. I swear, I don't know. Awwwww!" he hollered again.

Hood Rich took the knife and yanked it down his thigh, opening the gash in his leg so wide that I could see his bloody meat. Then he took the knife out and slammed it into his other thigh.

"I'm gon' ask yo punk ass one more time. Where is Meech and who gave the orders for niggaz to run in my trap houses?" He leaned on the knife's handle, forcing it to lodge itself deeper into Poppa's thigh.

Poppa leaned his head back as tears ran down his face. He was shaking so bad by this point that I thought he was having a mini seizure. Blood ran down his legs and there was a puddle of it under his chair.

Beside him, the female started to shake and piss on herself. I could hear her crying underneath her tape.

"Uhhh! Uhhh! I ain't never been no snitch, Hood Rich. I ain't never told on a nigga a day in my life. Now, I know how you get down. You gon' kill me anyway whether I tell you where that nigga, Mccch, at or not. So, fuck that. I ain't telling you shit. You might as well gon' and kill me and get this shit over with."

Hood Rich looked back over his shoulder at me. "You hear this fuck nigga. This nigga think I ain't finna get what I want. A'ight, we gon' see about that right now." He took a step back and kicked him in the chest so hard that he fell backward, then Hood Rich knelt beside him and yanked his boxers down. "You think you got kahunas, huh? You got balls, my nigga. A'ight, well, let me cut these bitchez off one at a time." He put his knees on Poppa's neck roughly. "You see all you niggaz must have forgot who ran Chicago. It wasn't none of them gang niggaz. It's always been Hood Rich ever since I took over the Stateway Projects."

He grabbed Poppa's nuts roughly in his hands, squeezing them with all his might.

"Arrrgh! Arrrgh!" Poppa shook his head from side to side. "Don't do this shit, Hood Rich. Please! I'm begging you!" he hollered, twisting on the floor to no avail because Hood Rich had his knee in his throat.

The words that he hollered were barely coherent. After each one, there were the sounds of him choking on his own spit and Hood Rich's knee.

Hood Rich looked back at me. "Come here, lil' homie, because I want you to see this shit live and direct. When you fucking with me, this how we gotta get down or niggaz a take advantage of our status. The more money you get that's the softer they think you become. But not Hood Rich. Never that, and not you either, Taurus. I'm gon' make sure of that shit."

He squeezed Poppa's nuts, then he raised the knife and brought it down at full speed right into the center of his testicles. Pinning them to the ground below us. As soon as I saw that blade connect with his sack, I closed my eyes because just looking at it happen made it feel like it was happening to me. I cringed.

"Arrrgh! Arrgh! Arrrgh! Help me! Help me! Somebody please!" He screamed like a bitch and I understood his pleas.

For the first time in my life, I actually understood why a nigga was screaming like a ho. I opened my eyes and shook my head.

The female was shaking so hard in her seat that I could hear that chair knocking against the floor. Hood Rich took the knife and sliced it down the middle of his sack, then he pulled the knife to the right, stood up, placed the toe of his Gucci boots on one of the balls and drug it across the floor, tearing it from Poppa's body.

"One down one more to go. Where is Meech?"

Poppa's eyes rolled into the back of his head and he passed out.

Smack!

I hit him so hard that I felt my elbow go numb.

"Arrrgh! Arrgh!" Blood dripped out of the corners of his mouth. There was so much sweat on his forehead that it looked like he'd just got done playing a full game of basketball in the summer sun. He smacked his lips together, as the blood continued to pour out of his middle as if he were on his period. "He fucking around in St. Louis now, with some nigga named Mello. They flooded the Lou' with The Rebirth and them niggaz up there doing numbers. Mello a savage just like y'all, Hood Rich. He 'bout that life. You'll see. Meech gave the word for yo houses to be knocked off. He say they under new management. He got them Jews funding him with whatever he need. Now kill me. I can't take this shit no more. Please, man!" he hollered, with blood dripping from his chin.

Hood Rich leaned over into his face. "Bitch ass nigga, is that it? You telling me everything right now?" he asked.

Poppa nodded his head. "That's everything, Hood Rich. Kill me, bruh, I'll see you in hell real soon."

Hood Rich handed me the knife. "Kill that fool, lil' bruh. I'll handle this bitch." He walked over to her chair and put his arm around her neck, squeezing as hard as he could.

I flipped Poppa on his stomach, sat on his back and pulled his head back using his hair. Then I took the knife, placed it at the left side of his throat, leaned his head forward and slit it with all my might. His blood sprayed across the floor. I got up and looked down on him, listening to the constant gurgling of him choking on his own blood, before he was dead as a corpse.

Hood Rich choked out the woman, then he laid her on her back and we got out of there. I was thankful that we didn't have to kill all of those lil' girls because if we had, I wasn't sure if I would have been able to follow through with it.

After we left Poppa's house, we wound up going to the Wild Hunnits of Chicago, where Hood Rich had his goons kick in an apartment door, before we came in behind them on business.

Chapter 4

By the time we got into the apartment, there were about ten young niggaz laid on their stomachs with Hood Rich's goons standing over them with assault rifles. Hood Rich walked into the kitchen where they were all laid out with roaches crawling all over the floor.

The house smelled rank, like weed smoke and funk. There wasn't any furniture inside of it, other than five blue milk crates and a big screened television that was connected to an X-box.

On the floor, in the living room, was a table with no legs. On top of it was a bunch of aluminum foiled heroin and sandwich bags. In the kitchen, beside each of the dudes were hand pistols that I guessed Hood Rich's men had taken from them and placed beside them to taunt them in such a way.

Hood Rich snatched up one of the lil' niggaz, some fat dude with long dreds. He slammed his face against the wall and put a .45 in his mouth so far that the young nigga started to gag.

"Ack! Ack! Uhhh! Uhh!"

"Fuck nigga. I been feeding you and yo family since yo punk ass came out the womb and this how you repay me? Crossing me for that weak ass nigga, Meech?" He smacked him with the banger and threw him to the floor.

The fat nigga scooted backward on his ass. "Chief! Chief, I ain't did shit. I honor you over that nigga, Meech. I always have," he said with his eyes wide open.

Hood Rich stepped forward and put the pistol to his forehead.

"How you honor me when you gave the order for yo stick up kids to hit my trap houses, nigga, and don't say it wasn't you because they used the Mach .90's with the noise reductions that I gave yo punk ass three weeks before them licks happened. That's what you call honor? Huh?" He pressed the barrel harder into his head. Lowering his eyes into slits.

The fat nigga closed his eyes and swallowed. "I'm sorry, man. I swear to God I'm sorry. It's just that nigga, Meech, got me doing that Rebirth shit and I can't think straight. He got control of my mind, man. I'll do anything he say and not because I fear him, but I fear him cutting off my supply of The Rebirth. I'm in too deep, Hood Rich. I can't control what I do no more, man." He whimpered, and I got ready to kick him in the chest. I hated whiney niggaz. That shit irritated me so bad that it made me want to scream.

Hood Rich grabbed him by the neck. "Who is Mello? When that nigga start coming down to The Land? When did him and Meech link up?"

The fat nigga swallowed. "Mello from St. Louis. He fuck with them Haitian niggaz out that way. Some heavy hittas from the mother land. Most of them niggaz don't even speak English, just hollering in French and shit. Meech moved The Re-birth out that way and Mello plugged him a cargo of bitchez coming from the islands. Meech fucking around in the sex game now. Say its millions. Got bitchez fucking and transporting dope in they bodies. It's crazy, but the homie on a whole 'nother level from where y'all left off. He even got young bitchez out here pounding the pavement. Everybody addicted to The Rebirth. Meech got our minds, man, and our bodies."

Hood Rich grunted. "When the next time that nigga supposed to show up to make a drop off to you? Huh?" he asked with a harsh tone.

The fat nigga shrugged his shoulders. "He got lil' nobody ass niggaz to do that now. The homie too major to drop off anything. He got a lil' crew that call themselves Duffle Bag Gettaz, they from the Ada B. Wells Projects. It's about twenty of them lil' niggaz. They stay with bangers and do anything that Meech tell 'em. If any-body knows when the next time he coming to town or where that nigga at, its them because he gotta pick up his bags of money from them weekly. I got fifty stacks in the safe that Lil' June Bug gon' be coming to get in two days. He takes that paper straight to Meech. That I know for a fact," he said, looking down at the barrel of the gun nervously.

The other lil' dudes were moving around uncomfortably on the floor. There were roaches crawling all over them and more than once I'd seen a few rats scurrying against the wall trying to stay out of view with no success.

"Give me they direct address, lil' nigga, and tell me who calling for them over there?" Hood Rich ordered through clenched teeth. He wrapped the fat dude's shirt into his fist and held his body a few inches from the roach infested floor.

"It's 3749 South Drexel. That's the buildings they operate out of. The nigga that's calling for them name is June Bug just like I just said. Just tell him that you coming to drop off that fifty bands and he gon' let you up." The fat dude swallowed. "A'ight, man, that's everything. Let me go now, Hood Rich. I swear I'ma fall in line."

Boom! Boom!

Hood Rich took a step back and aimed the gun down at the fat nigga again.

Boom! Boom!

All fours shots chopped into his face and left his plasma leaking out of the back of his skull.

"A'ight now listen up, you lil' bitch ass niggaz. I know where every last one of you lil' niggaz stay and where your mother and grandmother's stay. Muhfuckas go to the law and its gon' be a problem. Do I make myself clear?" he asked, walking around their bodies. There was a bunch of murmuring in the room. I could tell that the lil' dudes were terrified that they were going to be next. He snatched up a dark-skinned dude with short dreads and threw him against the wall, putting the pistol to his head. "Yo name Trell, right?"

The boy nodded his head. "Yeah, man, that's my name. What I do to you?" he asked, looking Hood Rich in the eyes with no fear, it seemed. He even curled his up-per lip.

"Yo morns was addicted to that shit on her way out of the game, before I snatched her up and put her in rehab. Then I put them bands in yo pocket and helped you and yo lil' sister eat. Didn't I put y'all in a nice lil' apartment on Bishop?" he asked, looking him over closely.

Trell nodded. "Yeah, man, I'd never forget that. My moms back in church and she don't fuck with that shit no more. My sister going to Notre Dame next semester. She been on the honor roll ever since we left behind them projects." He swallowed.

Hood Rich nodded. "Yeah, that's how it's supposed to work. Now be honest with me. Did you have anything to do with my traps being hit? Did you rollout with this dead ass nigga?" he asked, poking the dead fat dude with the toe of his boot.

Trell shook his head. "Never! I got loyalty inside my DNA. I would never cross you, Hood Rich. Word is bond. I was looking for an opening to hit that nigga right there. I was gon' wait until my sister was away at college, that way I wouldn't have to worry about her being a target of Meech 'nem. But nall, I'd never fuck you over like that. That's on my mother's strength," he swore, hitting his chest.

Hood Rich leaned forward and looked into his eyes. "What about any other nigga that's in this room. Keep that shit one hunnit, and don't feel like no snitch either. Matter fact." Hood Rich opened his fatigue jacket and took a .45 out of the holster, cocked it back and handed it to Trell. "Lil homie, anyone of these niggaz that's in here that ran into one of my traps or crossed me in any way that you know of, I want you to body they ass, right here and right now. That fifty gees that this dead nigga got in that other room is yours, plus them kilos on the table out there. I'll give you a slot in my mob and make sure that yo people ain't never gotta worry about eating no more. You hear me?" Hood Rich said, lowering his eyes into slits.

Trell looked him over for a long time in silence. "Man, fuck these niggaz. I gotta make sure my sister and mother stay straight. These punks ain't loyal anyway." He turned around and stood over one dude who had his face in his arms while he laid on his stomach. "He ran in one."

Boom! Boom!

The boy's body leaped from the floor, then he turned over and bled out. Trell curled his upper lip and walked to the boy next to that one. The boy tried to get up with his hands in front of him.

"Trell! Trell! You my nigga, fam! You my…"

Boom! Boom!

The boy flew against the wall, holding his face as blood oozed through his fingers.

Boom!

Trell finished him with one to the chest. He slumped over and fell to the kitchen floor in a pile of roaches. Instead of them scattering, they crawled over to his body and started to run all over it. The two rats that were by the wall slowly made their way to the fat dude's body and began to gnaw away at that. Then three came from out of the bathroom and pitter pattered their way alongside the other rats that were already feasting on his remains.

I shuddered at the sight because it made my flesh crawl. Even the rodents in Chicago were grimey and heartless.

Trell leaned down and snatched up one kid that couldn't have been older than fourteen years old. He wrapped his fist in his shirt and slammed him against the wall just like Hood Rich had done him. They boy started to plead for his life right away.

"Please don't kill me, Trell, I'm sorry. I'll do anything, man. I was just doing what my brother told me to do. I, uh, uh, ack!"

Trell forced the gun down the boy's throat. "This my lil' cousin, Hood Rich, but he was with them niggaz. If you saying I gotta hit everybody, well, he the last one here that was with them niggaz that tore off a few of yo traps. He only thirteen. man. Just tell me what to do," Trell said, looking over his shoulder at Hood Rich.

I immediately placed myself in his position. I didn't know if I would have smoked one of my loved ones just because another nigga wanted me too. I felt like Trell was caught between a rock and hard place. He wanted to make sure that his mother and sister were taken care of and he knew Hood Rich was the nigga to make sure that happened.

I was curious to see what was going to take place. There were three more dudes on the floor, crying into their arms. I wanted to know what was going to happen to them because at this point, there had been too many murders committed to just let them walk away scot free.

Hood Rich scrunched his face. "Fuck that lil' nigga. Meech was more than my blood and when I catch him, that ain't gon' mean shit. I'm splashing that punk. So, you do what you gotta do."

Trell blinked tears, then he took a deep breath.

"Please. Please don't do this. Please, I'm…"

Boom!

His head jerked on his shoulders, before he fell to the ground with his brains splashed across his face.

He turned around to face Hood Rich and Hood Rich took his .45 and slammed it to Trellis forehead.

Boom! Boom!

Trell fell backwards and bussed two times. His bullets hitting the ceiling, before he landed on his side in a puddle of blood.

Hood Rich walked over to the remaining dudes and gunned them down while I stood there watching the shit play out like a good ass movie.

The kitchen smelled like blood, piss and feces. Rats started to come out of everywhere, as if they were used to murder. As if it were an invitation for them to feast until they burped repeatedly.

That night we stayed in the Hilton downtown, in a pent-house suite that had six of the baddest Spanish chicks had ever seen in my life, and I'd seen some that were so bad that I couldn't stop looking, even with Princess pinching the shit out of me.

I took the last bite of my Lobster, chewed it with my eyes closed, then I grabbed a bottle of strawberry Cîroc, sipping while on of the Spanish broads massaged my shoulders and occasionally kissed on my neck.

"You almost ready for me, Papi?" she asked, leaning forward and planting an-other kiss on my neck, before sucking it like a Vampire. She was so strapped that every time she walked around the room, I couldn't take my eyes off her.

Her hair was long and curly. It dropped to her waist. I didn't know if it was real and I didn't care. She looked good with it.

I smiled. "Baby I'm still thinking about it. I mean but you can earn this dick if you 'bout that life." I flirted. I was having a tough time not taking this chick down.

Images of what it would feel like to be deep in her womb flooded my mind causing my dick to stand at attention. I would fuck her with everything I had in me and break her lil' ass down. I swore that fucking bad bitchez was the best 'cuz I always made it my business to treat they ass. I wanted them to get up from the bed with me with their mind blown.

"Awwwa, Papi," she whined, then she came around and sat on my lap, with her back to my chest. She situated herself in my lap, then she slowly started to wind. Her big booty was grinding on my dick. The scent of her perfume going up my nose. The hint at her femininity was driving me crazy.

In front of us, Hood Rich stood in the Jacuzzi with two of the broads kissing all over his lips and each other, while the other one dropped down in the pool and pulled his dick out of his Polo boxers, stroking it back and forth, before sliding it into her mouth, while she rubbed on the other two Rican's asses, slipping her hands between their legs, then sliding her fingers into their naked pussies from the back.

I watched them arch their backs and bend over a little bit while they continued to attack Hood Rich, moaning loudly.

The Rican in my lap had grabbed my hand and put it into her panties. I rubbed over her naked lips, then I slid two of my fingers into her box, dipping them in and out, while she moaned at the top of her lungs.

"Ay, Papi! Ay, mi Amor! Papi! Papi! Oh, mi Amor! Mi Amor!" she screamed, humping her hips into my hand again and again and again.

Hood Rich bent one of the chicks over the Jacuzzi, smacked her on the ass, then he took his dick out of the other one's mouth to slide deep into the one bent over.

She scrunched her face. "Fuck me, Hood Rich. Give me that dick, Papi! I wanna prove to them how you be fucking me. Then I want you to fuck my sisters the same way. Uhhh!" she screamed.

Hood Rich grabbed her hair roughly and got to pounding her with all his might. Her titties bounced back and forth. Both nipples erect.

One of the other Ricans stepped in front of her, sat on the edge of the Jacuzzi and spread her thighs wide before forcing her face into her pussy. It was like she al-ready knew what it was because she started to eat her monkey right away, tearing that shit up.

The one being eaten threw her head back and moaned at the top of her lungs while another one rubbed all over her titties and pulled on her nipples.

The one in my lap had her panties being pulled down, and off her ankles. The Ri-can in front of us squatted down and got to eating her pussy, while I rubbed all over her titties and bit into her neck.

"Tell me what she doing, baby. Tell me how that shit feel?" I growled reaching down and holding her pussy lips apart for her. The chick down there was going so crazy that she was licking my fingers and her pussy. I pinched her clit and that made her nearly jump out of my lap. Her juices were all over the both of us.

"Unn. Unn. Ay! Ay! Yes! Yes! Oh, fuck yes! Eat me, Manuela! Eat me, mi Hermana! I love it! Unnn! I'm cumming! I'm cumming Manuela!" She screamed, grabbed her head and wrapped her thick thighs around it, while I pulled on her nipples and sucked on her neck so hard that I left marks all over it.

Hood Rich was out of the Jacuzzi and laying on his back. He had one Rican sitting on his face, one riding his dick and the other one with her face between their legs sucking and licking up their sex juices.

There was another Rican who sat on the edge of the Jacuzzi fingering herself at full speed. Sweat poured down the side of her face and onto her heavy breasts. The room smelled like spicy pussy. I wanted to fuck two of them lil' hoez so bad but I didn't because I had Princess on my mind like crazy.

I watched Hood Rich fuck all six of them hoez and we didn't kick them out until five in the morning. Had they ass dropped off by limo, then me and the homie passed out, me in the bed and him on the couch.

I woke up seven hours later right around noon. Hood Rich was already up and on his phone. When he saw that I was awake, he grabbed the hotel phone and ordered me a steak, triple cheesed omelet, hash browns and a pitcher of Orange juice. I ate my breakfast while he broke shit down for me.

"Look, Taurus. I wanna go hit them niggaz out there in the Ada B. Wells tonight, but I think we need to let the city cool off, so I'ma chill. I got some bitness that I need to handle over there in Indiana that's gon' take me about three days to get shit in order, then we gon' shoot out to Houston and I'ma hand you over Clover City in front of Flip and Screw. Then niggaz have been bought out and they gon' work un-der you. Understand that?" he asked, inhaling smoke from his Cuban cigar that was filled with Tropical Loud.

I nodded. "Man, Hood Rich I ain't trying to be in this hotel for no three days. If you going next door to Indiana, then let me shoot back home to Dallas, so I can check on Princess and Jahliya."

The last thing I needed was to be cooped in that hotel with my mind going a million miles a minute. I needed to check on Princess. She'd not left me one text and that wasn't like her.

On the other hand, Blaze had left me ten and I'd yet to respond to either of them. But I knew she'd saw that I read them.

Hood Rich nodded. "Look, today is Sunday, I'ma let you fly the jet back to Dallas so you can handle yo bitness. Take three days off. I'll hit you up on Wednesday and have you fly back out this way Thursday in the middle of the night just like before. By that time, I should have more in-formation, and be ready to move forward with this quest to find Meech punk ass. Go get yo shit in order and we'll ro-tate in a minute. Remember, after you rest, we back on bit-ness. We hit up a few more of these niggaz out this way, then shoot over to Houston and conquer Clover City. It's time you get yo chips up. It's good money out there, trust me."

Chapter 5

I got back to Dallas three hours later and twenty minutes after I touched down. I was at the crib kissing a sleeping Jahliya on the cheek. I put her pink Burberry blanket over her, then I stepped out of her room, leaving the door open a lil' bit.

Princess was in the living room, vacuuming the carpet with SZA playing in the back ground. I walked up to her from behind and wrapped her in my arms. I needed to feel some sort of affection from her because she had not been emotionally open for me ever since I'd told her about Blaze being pregnant.

I was hoping the information didn't ruin our relationship. I loved her more than anybody in the world, that included my daughter and my mother. I kissed her on the neck and she jerked her head away as if she were repulsed by me. That hurt my heart.

"Ugh, get away from me, Taurus. I ain't in the mood for that right now. You think I forgot about what the fuck you told me before you left here a few days ago." She scrunched her face, then she shook her head.

I stood there, in the middle of the carpet in silence, irritated and hurt at the same time. She kept right on vacuuming as if she didn't see me standing there stuck. I went and stood in front of her cleaning path.

"Move!" She hollered, waving me off. "Get out of my fuckin' way." Then she had the nerve to run over my foot. I jumped back and mugged her with anger. "Told yo ass to move."

I walked over to the wall and yanked the cord to the vacuum cleaner out. "Instead of you moping around with an attitude why don't you talk to me about this shit and tell me what's on yo mind. We're too grown for these games, Princess, seriously. It's too much shit going on in our lives that I need to handle, and I don't have the time to be worried about what kind of vindictive shit you gon' be on. So, be a woman and tell me what's good?" I asked, looking down on her.

She flung the vacuum cleaner to the floor and stepped into my face. Poking me in the chest with her little finger. "You got that bitch pregnant, that's what the fuck my problem is, nigga. That and the fact that you ain't trying to have this bitch get rid of that kid. I ain't trying to be sharing you with this bitch when I'm sixty and ain't down for threesomes no more. I ain't trying to have my daughter have no half siblings either. She deserves all of you, all the time, because you barely here as it is. Always out handling something." She did air quotes. "This better be the only bitch you got pregnant, too, Taurus. I swear to God if I find out you got any other kids besides my daughter and that bitch's, nigga I'm whacking yo ass. Then, it's ova for me because as crazy as it is, I refuse to be in this world if you ain't in it. Now the fact that I'm walking around quiet and ain't kilt nobody should be a good thing for you 'cuz I'm tellin' you, I'm inches away from findin' Blaze and killin' that bitch and cuttin' her uterus out. You think this shit is a game, but you must've forgot how I did Juice's pregnant bitch." She glared at me, then bumped me out of the way as hard as her lil' body could and picked up the vacuum cleaner's cord, getting ready to plug it into the wall.

I looked at her from the corner of my eyes for a long time, feeling my heart pounding in my chest. I felt like Princess was testing me to my very core. It was taking everything in me to not snatch her ass up. She had me beyond heated.

I exhaled loudly and walked out of the room, heading to our bedroom. I sat on the bed, trying to clear my head when my phone buzzed. It was a message from Blaze.

Blaze: I'm still out here, Taurus, because I'm missing you so bad. Fuck that dancing shit. I just wanna be with you and in your arms for as long as you'll allow me to be. Hit me back.

Me: on my way

I know a nigga wrong, but I had to go see about her. I got fitted in Ferragamo. While I was getting dressed, Princess didn't utter a word. She just kept on cleaning the crib in silence. I wanted to go over and hug her. Just to feel her body heat against mine. I needed to hear her tell me that she loved me like she always had. But I knew wasn't none of that jumping off. Anytime I was around or a part of so much killing, afterward I needed to be in the presence of a woman just to bring me back down to earth.

I'd been that way ever since my first kill and the woman I had turned too was my mother. It was my only way to keep from going crazy.

Most people thought after a person killed another that it was just over, but that wasn't the case, at least not for me. Every time I killed somebody their spirit would hang around on me for months. Haunting my dreams, my thoughts, everything. I'd see their images out of the corners of my eyes. It got to the point that it was hard for me to think straight, so I healed myself through the presence and body of a woman.

I stepped to the front door and got ready to leave out of it, just as Princess walked past and into the kitchen. She didn't even look my way.

"Princess, I'm finna step out for a minute. I'll be back in a few hours, if that's cool with you. I mean, unless you need me to take care of somethin' here."

She turned around and looked me up and down. "What you telling me for? I don't give a fuck what you do as long as that bitch got yo baby in her, I'm numb to the shit, so you ain't gotta tell me shit. Word is bond." She gave me a disgusted look and shook her head.

I swallowed. "On some real shit, all them comments you makin' breakin' me down 'cuz I love you so fucking much. You don't know what I been through out there in Chicago. I need to chill with my woman and be loved for a minute. All that rough and rugged shit need to be out the window."

She shrugged her shoulders. "You love me, but yo pathetic ass need to 'step out for a minute'," she mimicked me, "rather than to be here and make shit right. Just like a nigga. Make shit all about y'all 'cuz y'all *hurt so bad*. Fuck outta here." She waved me off. "But, you a good lookin' nigga, Taurus, and you got plenty money. I'm pretty sure you can find some bitch that wanna be all under you right now 'cuz I don't. Lookin' at you makes me sick to my stomach. Ona real tho, I need you to stay away for a while. I need some space." She shook her head and turned her back on me. "I'on't give a fuck what you do."

I don't know why her comments were killing me so much, but they were. Everything she said felt like a bullet to my gut.

I could barely breathe. I mean, this was my princess. My rider. She rode beside me in New York and in Memphis while we brought them cities to their knees. Now she was making it seem like she didn't even care about me anymore, and that was murdering me.

I felt the lump in my throat and swallowed again. "Princess, I know you don't mean what you sayin' right now. You just going through it 'cuz of this whole pregnancy thing, so I'm not gon' hold them words you sayin' out of yo mouth against you. But jus' know that everything you sayin' is killing my soul. You breakin' me down right now."

She looked me up and down and shrugged her shoulders. "I don't care. Maybe if I break you down far enough you'll be at eye level to me and you can see how this shit feels." She turned her back and started to unload the dishwasher.

***

Blaze had got a suite at the Waldorf Astoria. Her room was huge and all-white. There was a big bed in the middle of the room with a thousand count Louis Vuitton sheets on it.

The carpet was real fluffy and when I stepped on to it, it felt like I was walking on a cloud. There was a six-person hot tub a few feet away from the bed and to the right of the hot tub was a ninety-inch smart television and sound system, which played jazz music.

To the left of the room, and about forty feet away from the door, was a roaring fire place. That is where I found myself, sitting in front of, hugged up with Blaze while she laid her head back on my chest.

I wrapped my arms around her and breathed in the aroma coming from her scalp that smelled like coconut oil, and Prada perfume.

She rubbed my arms. "Baby, I'm so glad that you came. I ain't even gon' lie I didn't expect you too. I thought Princess was gon' lock yo ass down. I missed you so much."

She turned around and kissed me on the lips, sucking all over mine, before sliding her tongue into my mouth.

I kissed her back but didn't put all of me into it. She must have noticed because mid-kiss she stopped, opened her eyes and broke away from me, then she turned all the way around and knelt in front of me while I looked off avoiding her eye contact.

She took my face in between her hands. "What's the matter, baby? You're not yourself. Is it me?" she asked with a face full of concern and worry.

I shook my head. Looking into her beautiful face. Man, Blaze was bad.

Her skin was flawless, without make up. She had these lil' freckles that decorated her cheeks that one could call her only imperfection, but to me, it made her look that much colder.

She always smelled good. She was soft spoken, with a warm spirit. Being with Blaze since the first day I met her had always seemed like an escape from the slums and from my world of pain. She was my oasis. My paradise and every time I realized that, it scared me.

It scared me because I could see myself being with her, happily, and without drama. I knew that deep down that's what I wanted. But at the same time, I loved Princess so much. I could never see myself leaving her or being without her. I was so caught up that I didn't know what to do.

Blaze leaned forward and kissed my lips again. "It's okay, baby. You can tell me whatever is on your heart. I'm strong enough to take it. Please… just be honest." She rubbed the side of my face with her left hand, looking deep into my soul.

I grabbed her hands and held them. "Blaze, Princess ain't trying to honor you being pregnant. Ever since I told her, she been acting real funny toward me, like she hates me or somethin'. I love her so much and I really don't know what to do. Ever since she's been in my life, we been holding each other down through one tragedy after the next. For some reason, I feel like I'm betraying her or somethin'. I promised to never hurt her, but I feel like I am." I took a deep breath and exhaled, avoiding eye contact with her.

I knew what I'd said probably wasn't gon' sit well with her, but ever since I'd known her I'd never lied to her about anything. I just didn't operate like that. If I loved or cared about a female, I didn't lie to them under no circumstances. I cared about Blaze a lot. I saw myself possibly being with her on so many levels now that she was having my kid. I had a profound respect for her as a woman and the mother of my child-to-be.

Blaze turned my face once again, so she was looking me in the eyes. "Baby, listen to me. I understand how you feel about her and you need to know that it's okay. I'm not trying to take you away from her and keep you all to myself. I'm perfectly fine with having a piece of you. I love you that much, and so will our child." She rubbed her thumb along the side of my face and smiled weakly. Looking fine as hell. "Taurus, I'm crazy about you, and I'm not letting you go. I know that I can play my role and still hold you down like no other. I ain't trying to step on Princess' toes by any means, but if it came down to that, she can't compete with me on no level because I'm a grown ass woman. I ain't got time for those kiddy high school games. We just so happen to love the same man and we each have a child by him. I think she sees me as a threat because there is nothin' that she can really offer you. She sees me, and she knows that I am light years ahead of her on every level except that hood shit." She looked into my eyes and kissed my cheek. "I'll do anything for you, Taurus. Anything to prove that I am your one. Whatever role you need me to play, I'll play it, and I'll stick to the script. All I ask is that you love me when you're with me. We can even schedule the times we'll spend together if it'll make your home situation better. All I care is that I am a part of you, and you are a part of me and our child's life forever." I shook my head because Blaze was gaming the fuck out of me.

I knew that every word she spoke was more than likely the truth and it was making me fall for her so hard because she was being so one hunnit about the situation. That mature thing she had going was driving me nuts.

I looked over her face and she kept on getting finer and finer to me. I rolled my neck around on my shoulders.

"Blaze, I'ma keep shit really real with you. I love you like crazy. You ain't never brought no drama my way and the way you care about me means a lot to me, especially right now when I'm so broken down mentally. Like I really didn't know what to do when I got here, but now all I keep saying to myself is that I can't be away from you. I need you in my life. I need your unconditional love and guidance in this realm. I'm new at this shit and its killing me. I don't wanna hurt you or Princess. And I don't want to lose you or Princess."

She shook her head. "You'll never lose me. I'll never leave your side and whenever you call, I'll come running full speed and kneel in front of you in submission. Since day one, all I've wanted to do was pick you up and place you on a throne

that is all your own. You deserve the best, Taurus. I'll go broke making sure you have everything you want in life. You're supposed to be a boss and I'm supposed to be at your right hand, next to the boss. You can give Princess anything she wants from you, just give me your mind and your ambition. Oh, and this too, but I'll share this with her," she said, grabbing ahold of my dick and squeezing it.

I don't know how she wound up on top of me but the next thing I knew, she was straddling me and rubbing some eatable oils all over my chest and abs. Then she leaned down and licked it up, biting certain parts of me, while SZA sang on in the back ground.

I placed my big hands on her booty and squeezed the cheeks, while she sat atop me and did her. She sat up for a second opening her bra from the front and unleashing them pretty titties. Both fell out of their cups, exposing themselves to me, with hard nipples that looked ready for action.

"Taurus, I know you used to beating this pussy in, but tonight I want us to make love. I mean, I ain't telling you to take it easy on me because I need that thug shit, but just for tonight when you're in me, feel how much I need you. How much I really, really love you and surrender my body to you on all levels. You are my king." She ran her tongue across her juicy lips, then she slid down my stomach, grabbing my dick and stroking it up and down before sliding it into her mouth and sucking me like a pro.

My eyes rolled into the back of my head, as I felt her nip at the head with her teeth purposely. That shit drove me crazy and I couldn't help making some weird ass noises.

She popped it out with a loud sucking noise. "You like that, baby. Tell me how much you like when I swallow this whole thang. How many of them hoez you got out there that can do yo body like me, Taurus? Be honest?" She sucked me back into her mouth and started to spear her head into my lap at a hundred miles an hour, making loud noises and moaning all around it.

Every now and then, she would pop it out just to tell me how much she loved me, and I couldn't lie, she was breaking me down emotionally because I was vulnerable as hell.

Most women didn't know that the best time to break down a man and get into his mental was when they were driving him sexually insane.

When we are at our highest sexual peak, that's when everything makes sense and our emotional arms are open and looking for a hug. If a woman wanted to play with a man's mind at any time, that was the best time.

Everything Blaze was saying to me was not only sticking, but it was weakening me for her. I felt myself needing her and wanting her more than ever. It was a feeling that I had only experienced with Princess and I never thought any female would get me there besides her.

She sucked me faster and faster, swallowing me with no hands. She had them laid at her sides, proving to me that she was a beast at her head game.

I closed my eyes, then I opened them, watching her doing me in. I pumped my hips into the air, making my dick hit the back of her throat again and again.

For the first time I noted that she had her fingers between her legs, moving them in and out of her at full speed. It was all I could take. Her breasts bounced on her chest and I felt her teeth nip at my head again before going to the back of her throat.

I grabbed her hair and then I was cumming in rivers down her throat.

"Awwww!" I hollered and humped into her mouth.

Only then did she grab my dick and get to pumping it up and down while it erupted inside of her mouth. "Ummm, yes. Ummm. Give me all them juices, baby. Umm-hmm."

She pumped it some more, squeezing me cum to the top of my dick, before sucking it off the head.

She straddled me again, reached under herself and tried to grab for my dick, but I flipped her on to her back and slid down her body. Stopping so I could kiss and suck on her neck.

Tasting her sweet perfume that was mixed with a little sweat, I bit into it and pulled up her skin with my teeth.

"Ummm, baby. Just me do right. Please. Please make love to me. I love you so much, Taurus. I belong to you. I belong to only you," she whimpered. I looked up into her face and saw the tears flowing down her cheeks.

I trailed my kisses down to her breasts, squeezing them together before sucking on one nipple and then the next. I tried not to be so rough knowing that she was pregnant, and her titties were already a little sore, but I was obsessed with her nipples, sucking on them as if they were my fetish. I just couldn't get enough.

"Yes, Taurus. Go lower, baby. Go lower. I want you to taste me."

Chapter 6

I pushed her knees to her chest and held them there while my face disappeared between her thighs, sucking her whole pussy into my mouth and sliding my tongue up and down her crease. She tasted salty and sweet at the same time. Her essence was driving me nuts.

"Umm. Umm. Yes, Taurus. Eat me, baby. Eat me. I love you so fucking much. I love you so much, baby. I belong to you!" she hollered.

I slurped up and down her crease, then I trapped her swollen clit with my lips and nipped at it with my teeth, only to suck on it some more and repeat the process. She threw her thick thighs on to my shoulders and wrapped her ankles around my neck. With her hands, she pushed my face deeper into her sex, humping my mouth.

"Yes! Yes! Yes! I'm 'bouta cum! Don't stop! Please don't stop, I'm bouta cum, baby! Uhhhh-shit!"

While she shook like crazy, I continued to nip at her clit, suckin' it, running my tongue from side to side and up and down, slurping her juices and swallowing them.

While she came all over my mouth, I continued to handle my business. She screamed at the top of her lungs, shook for what seemed like forty seconds before passing out with her legs wide opened.

I straddled her, put her left thigh on my shoulder and slid my dick home. Her pussy was super-hot and inviting. Sucking me in hungrily with one stroke, I slid in and hit rock bottom, then I pulled all the way back, only to give it back to her again.

I got a steady rhythm going, then I leaned down and kissed her lips, sucking all over them.

"I love you, too, Blaze. Urn. Urn. Urn. Urn. I can't front no more. Baby, I love you just as much as you love me. You're my baby. I mean that shit," I said, after taking deep breaths in between.

I sped up the pace a little bit and ran my thumbs all over her erect nipples, pulling them because I knew it drove her crazy.

"Uhhh! Taurus!" she screamed and started to shake her head from left to right while I started to beat that pussy up. I couldn't hold back no more. That savage got to corning out of me. Her pussy was so so good. I couldn't control myself. I never could around her for some reason. "You fuckin' me again, Taurus! You fuckin' me! Uhh-a! I thought! Aww, aww, aww! I thought you said. Unnn-a! You was gon'! You was gon, oooo-a! Make love to me! Uhhh-I'm cumming, baby. Oooo-a! I'm cumming again!"

I had both of her ankles on my shoulders, fucking her nice and fast, hitting the bottom every time.

I laid on my back while she rode me with tears coming down her face. I didn't really know why she was crying and I didn't ask. I just allowed myself to get lost in the moment.

Her box felt so good milking me. Her hot body on top of mine felt so right. Mentally, she had me in another dimension where all that mattered was her and the baby growing inside of her. I mean, I never once forgot about Princess and Jahliya, but for those few hours that me and Blaze did our thing, I was able to escape the heartache and pain that was my home life.

Once again, she had acted as my oasis.

After we did our thing, we wound up in the hot tub with her back to my chest and my arms wrapped around her protectively.

SZA continued to bellow out of the speakers and there was no other place that I'd rather had been in that moment.

"Taurus, you know you gotta get back to her or she gon' kill yo ass. I mean, I wish you could stay with me all night but we both know that it's dangerous. Right now, you must be smart because there are two children involved and a total of five hearts on the line. I don't know how we're going to make it through the next few years, but I just want you to know that I will never leave you and I will always be waiting on your return with arms wide open. You're my everything and I mean that from the bottom of my heart." She turned around and straddled me again. I could feel her sex lips against my stomach. "Handle yo bitness, baby, like a boss, and get back to me because I need you."

I left out thirty minutes later and made my way back home where I parked my car in the drive way and fell asleep listening to Jay-z's 444 album. I didn't wake up until I heard the locks pop. Off instinct I reached under my driver's seat and came up with a .44 automatic, pointing it at the figure that was opening the passenger's door ready to pull the trigger.

Princess sucked her teeth, then she opened the door all the way. "Taurus, put that gun down before one of them nosey ass neighbors see you and call the police. That's the last thing we need right now." She rolled her eyes and sat in the passenger's seat with her arms crossed in front of her breasts, nodding her head to one of Jay's tracks.

I sat the pistol on my lap and yawned, looking her over closely. "What's on yo mind, Princess? I know damn well you ain't came out here just to sit in my truck and nod yo head to Jay. What's good?"

She grunted and smiled, refusing to look my way. Then she shrugged her shoulders. "I don't know. I guess I just been missin' you like crazy. I don't like when we fight. I feel like we can get through anything together but if we allow ourselves to be broken apart by this world, then what do we really have? Why did we go through so much side by side only to quit on each other shortly thereafter? So, this is what I was thinking. I was wrong to try and force you to have that girl get an abortion. And I was wrong for not honoring my part in all this mess because for the most part I was right beside you when you was fucking that girl, which meant that when she got pregnant I was more than likely in the bed with y'all." She lowered her head and exhaled loudly. "I'm sorry for being so childish. I don't want to run you away, Taurus, and I know you was probably with her last night because who else would you be at the Waldorf Astoria with?" She looked me over knowingly. I snapped my head to look at her and she smiled. "You forget that your phone and this truck both have tracking devices in them. I know where yo ass is at all times." She shook her head. "But that ain't important. I kinda hope you was with her and not somebody else. The last thing I need is for you to be back out there fucking plenty hoez. I know when you get to doing that that you really don't love me no more and you're searching for my replacement." She looked up at me. "So, were you with her last night?"

I sighed and slowly nodded my head. "Yeah. I was going through some emotional battles deep within myself and I just needed to be in the company of some-body that cared about me because you wasn't feeling me at the time."

She raised her left eyebrow. "So, you go and run to her when you feel like you ain't getting what you need from me? Now do you think that's fair? And how would you feel if I had a nigga I could go lay-up with when I felt like you wasn't giving me what I needed? How would you react to that?" she asked calmly.

I couldn't stop my face from frowning as much as I tried too. I got to imagining some punk ass nigga with his arms around her and even though they were fully clothed in my head, I still found myself getting heated just because he was touching her in a consoling manner. I didn't want nobody touching her under no circumstances as hypocritical as that may have sounded.

"Princess, you already know that I ain't geeing for that shit. I'd murk that nigga quick and make you bury him with me."

She laughed, then her face turned into a scowl. "You can do whatever you wanna do but if I do it, then you wanna kill somebody. What type of shit is that?" I was quiet and looked out of my driver's window. She grabbed my right shoulder and forced me to turn in her direction. "Answer me, Taurus, because this shit don't make no sense!" She screamed with her eyes closed. When she opened them, they were red and seething anger.

I felt my heart speed up. She was pissing me off. I didn't feel like arguing that early in the morning. I was still wore out from Blaze and I was mentally was all over the place.

"Princess, look, I don't wanna have this conversation right now. All I can say is that you're right and I ain't got no legs to stand on. I was feeling some type of way yesterday, you wasn't fucking with me, she called. I knew she'd be a little more consoling and understanding, so I went to her and got what I needed. If you did the same thing with another nigga, I'd be heated, ready to kill somethin', but you'd be perfectly within your rights. That's it, that's all." I was getting a headache. I wanted to go in the house and lay down, on some real shit. All that drama was wearing me out.

Just then, I saw my mother come out of the house holding Jahliya, bouncing her up and down on her hip. It seemed that the sun shined directly on her, causing her long curls to glisten in the sunlight.

She must of saw me peeping her from a distance because she took Jahliya's hand and made her wave to me.

I smiled. "When she get here?"

Princess curled her upper lip and looked out of the window toward her. "She came early this morning. I called her, told her that I needed a break. Think I'm finna leave for a week or so. I just need to get out of here and clear my head. This shit with Blaze is really fucking me up." She sighed. "Tell me something, Taurus, and I want you to be honest."

I watched my mother dance around with Jahliya. I could see both of their dimples on their cheeks from where I was. I missed my mother so much, I couldn't wait to hug her.

"Okay."

She sighed again. "I don't even know why I'm asking you this question because the truth of it ain't gon' do nothin' but break me down. But, do you love Blaze?" She looked at me with those big brown eyes that always broke me down to my knees.

I continued to look out of the window at my mother. I wondered how she was doing. I'd not seen her physically in two months.

From my vantage point, she looked healthy and more beautiful than I'd ever seen her before. She'd gotten her weight back and everything.

Her thighs were on full display, along with her stomach because of the tube top she was wearing.

"Princess I don't wanna do this right now. Please can we talk about something else?" I said, without looking her way.

She reached and grabbed a hold of my chin, making me face her. Her cheeks were full of tears. They slid from her eyes and dripped from her chin onto her naked brown thighs.

"Taurus, please. I just need to know what I'm dealing with here. Be honest with me. Do you love Blaze?" she asked with her voice breaking up a lot.

I looked into the eyes of my princess, my beautiful baby girl and I wanted to lie to her. I wanted to tell her everything other than the truth, but I just couldn't lie to her. I never had, ever since we'd known each other, and I wasn't about to start this day.

I slowly nodded my head. "Yeah, I love her, Princess, but not as much as I love you and our daughter. I mean, with Blaze, it's just..."

She didn't even let me finish. She got out of the truck and slammed the door. Walked over to her Range Rover, got in and backed it down the driveway.

"Momma, I'll be in touch. You know what we talked about. Later." She hit her horn once, then she backed into the street and stormed away from the house without so much as looking in my direction.

I was sick. I started hitting her phone right away, it rung and rung.

My mother disappeared into the house, then she came back out holding it in the air with Jahliya still on her hip. She answered her phone and I hung mine up.

I sat in the living room with my head down, while my mother sat across from me holding Jahliya. I reached out for my daughter and she handed her to me. I kissed her pretty face right away and she smiled with her deep dimples and her long curly hair already falling to her shoulders. I knew she'd gotten that from my mother's side of the family because her whole side had long curly hair and deep dimples. Creoles from the heart of Tennessee.

"Why I ain't never met this Blaze y'all talking about? Now you got a baby with her and stuff. I feel like I been left out of the loop," my mother said, rubbing my cheek with her soft fingers.

I shrugged my shoulders. "Me and her been off and on. We weren't really a thing, just sexing and then she got pregnant. I think Princess over reacting. Ever since she came into the picture, we both been screwing Blaze. So, when she got pregnant that means that she got some of her that day as well," I sighed. "I don't know, but all this is driving me crazy."

My mother sat on the couch and laid her head on my shoulder, then she looked up and kissed me on the cheek. "Its gon' be okay, baby. Momma here now and you already know that I got you. We're all that we got. Princess will be back. She just need some space. That lil' girl loves you to death, so I can't see her walking out of you and Jahliya's life. She's more of a woman than that. You just gotta figure out who you're going to be with, especially if you're in love with both. That's tricky." She kissed my cheek, then she laid her head back on my shoulder. "I missed you so much. I couldn't wait to see you and my grandbaby, Taurus. Have you missed me?"

I nodded, turned my head to the left and kissed her on the forehead and felt her shake underneath me as if my kiss was getting the better of her.

After I showered, I got Jahliya ready because I decided I was going to spend the whole day with my daughter. I just wanted to take her out and spoil her. I wanted to let her know how much her daddy really loved her, so the first place we went was Toys R Us.

I put her down in the little girls' aisle and let her run up and down it. Anything that she stopped in front of or tried to pull off the shelves, I got it and bought it for her, which was crazy because it seemed like she wanted to play with damn near everything in the store, but I didn't care. If she touched it, I bought it. I arranged for everything to be priority shipped to us. Once it got to our house, I would set it all up in her massive play room in the basement.

From there, I took her to Saks Fifth Ave and went nuts buying her all the latest clothing and shoes. Anything that looked pretty to me, that was hot, I copped it for her from each designer and got her a pair of shoes or sandals to go with it.

Then I took my baby to Kay's Jewelers and snatched her up some more diamonds for her ears and some small rings that wouldn't slide off her fingers. I made sure that the jeweler sized her fingers before I bought over ten gees worth of his merchandise for her.

Jahliya loved her some cheese pizza, so from there we went to Chuck E. Cheese and I bought her a large cheese pizza.

While it was cooling off, I let her wear herself out running around, playing in the ball pit, dancing with the mouse and his entourage on stage. She chased a bunch of white kids and they chased her. More than once, she fell, and I had to console her while she cried on my shoulder. Then I kissed her little knees and sat her back down. She ran away and started to play again, every once and a while looking back over her shoulder at me to make sure I was still there.

After that, she sat in my lap while she ate the cheese off the pizza with her hand. I mean, she got down. There was sauce and cheese all over her face and her Burberry bib. She also managed to get it into her hair, which I still couldn't figure that out because I was sitting right there holding her the whole time. But I wound up taking her into the bathroom and washing her up real good before we left.

We wound up at the beach, just as the sun was threatening to go down. I laid her on my chest and held her as she slept, snorin' just a little bit.

Holding her melted my heart and made me miss Princess like crazy. I wondered where she was and what was on her mind. Did she hate me now and would we ever be able to be back to the place we were six months ago?

I was lost in deep thought on the way home. Jahliya was in the back, in her car seat, out like a light.

I had the sounds of Jhene Aiko singing through the speakers and I was trying to get a hold of my mental and count my blessing. Things could have been a lot worse.

There was still the whole mission with Hood Rich that I needed to be prepared for and I only had one more night to do so. I didn't know what it would entail, but I couldn't wait to get it over and done with.

I shook my head and sighed. I picked up my phone, getting ready to text my mother to let her know I was on my way home.

I was about to slow down at the intersection, thinking that the light would flip yellow before I got there, but was surprised when it remained green all the way until I passed it. I looked down at my phone and started to text my mother.

Me: On my way home now, Ma, should be there in about…

Bam!

All I heard was metal crunching as my truck was hit from the side so hard that it started to flip over and repeatedly while sparks shot up from it.

Chapter 7

Jahliya screamed at the top of her lungs, as the masked men yanked me out of the windshield and threw me in a black van, with blood running down my face. I was dizzy and could barely see straight. A fist came at me full speed, ringing my belly, then I felt the pistol crack me in the side of the head and I was out like a light.

I was jarred awake an hour later by the feeling of being smacked so hard. I woke up hollering at the top of my lungs. My hands were cuffed and linked to a chain that led to my feet, which were shackled. On each side of me was a big beefy white wrestler looking man with shot guns to each of my temples. I wouldn't dare move.

"Wake up, Taurus! Wake the fuck up now, you black son of a bitch!" Serge hollered, with his face beet red, as a result.

I was out of breath. I struggled against my binds and tried to break free. "Where the fuck is my daughter?" I spat, with blood oozing out of my mouth. It hurt to talk. I felt like my jaw was broken or something.

Serge walked up to me and smacked me again so hard that I passed back out, then he smacked me awake. My neck snapped hard to the right, causing me to see blue lightning.

"You dirty black son of a bitch! Where is Nastia? I know you've been in contact with her because for some reason she's obsessed with you. Now, where is she?" He snarled, looking me up and down.

I shook my head. "I ain't heard from her, Serge. I ain't talked to her in almost a month. Last time I did, she wasn't even in the country. Said she'd get in contact with me when she was," I said, short of breath. It felt like my chest was caved in.

I struggled to breath, wheezing and everything. He swung and punched me in the ribs, then the stomach, then the ribs again, letting loose a flurry of blows that fucked

me up and had me hunched over coughing up blood. I hated his bitch ass, and I swore that one day I was going to kill him.

"You're a liar! She's been shipping so much dope to your ghettos that I know you must be pulling the strings." He grabbed me by the throat and squeezed. "You know where she is and you're going to find her, Taurus! You're going to find her right away or I'm going to make your life a living hell. Do you hear me? Hell!" he spat all into my face.

If it was one thing that I hated, it was when somebody spoke so close to me that they wound up spitting on me. But when they spit in my face, it made me want to kill them.

This bitch ass Russian sprayed me with his words and it made me both sick on the stomach and mad as a muthafucka. I lowered my eyes as I imagined myself chopping his bitch ass up.

He backhanded me, shocking the shit out of me, then he grabbed me by my shirt. "Do you hear me, motherfucker! Do you?" he hollered. I felt the blood sliding down my cheek and along my neck. I hated that muthafucka. It was hard for me to bow down and answer his questions and I think he must have sensed that, because he put his hand into the air and snapped his fingers. "Bring me that little bitch. I know how to get his attention," he ordered, before stepping away from me.

I raised my head in time to see a big beefy white dude with a little ass wife beater on walk from out of the shadows, holding Jahliya in his massive arms. I noticed that her mouth was taped, and she was throwing a fit while he held her in his arms.

Finally, he wrapped his fist into her clothes and handed her over to Serge roughly, as if she were a doll instead of a living person. Serge snatched her up, went into his waist and came up with a long sharp Army knife. He put her back against the wall and brought the knife to her throat.

"I swear, I'll cut this little whore's throat out of her if you don't answer me! Are you going to find my daughter or are you going to watch everybody around you be murdered one by one until you get it through your head that you don't run anything, you filthy black son of a bitch! Answer me!" he began to saw into her neck slowly, I saw traces of blood forming around the blade.

I knew from experience that Serge had no problems killing a child. He'd murdered both mine and my right-hand man, Tywain's, children less than two years ago.

"Okay! Okay! Serge, man, I'll do whatever you want. Just don't hurt my lil' girl, man. Please. Just tell me what you want me to do and I'll do it," I said, watching tears roll down Jahliya's face, with blood down her neck.

He frowned up at her. "I'll kill her, Taurus. You know I will. I'll kill her and won't lose one wink of sleep. I'm tired of playing games with you Americans. My daughter has been defiled by you people. Doing everything to uplift you and forget-ting about her own sacred Russian blood line. Do you know how many problems she's caused me ever since you came into the picture? Do you?" he hollered and cut Jahliya a little more.

I felt my stomach turn over. I felt like I was ready to throw up. I started to imagine the way he'd cut up my son in front of me, or at least the boy that Shakia was saying was my son.

Tremarion had been his name, and he'd not even made it to his first year on earth before Serge took his life in a bloody fashion. I couldn't let that happen to Jahliya. I was ten times crazier about my daughter than I had been the little boy.

When I looked at Jahliya, I saw Princess. I had to save my baby.

I shook my head. "Look, Serge, I don't know what she's done, man, but I'll find her. I swear, I will. You don't have to hurt my little girl. Just give me a little time and I'll have her sitting in front of you. You have my word."

Serge lowered her from the wall and walked across the warehouse until he was standing in front of me with a menacing look on his face. "Taurus, I'm giving you one week to have my daughter sitting in front of me. You have one week from today. One week and that's it. If you do not have her sitting in front of me by then, I will make your worst nightmares come true. You have my word on that."

***

I couldn't believe that this arrogant ass white man actually dropped me and Jahliya off at home and pushed us both out of his limo.

"One week, son of a bitch. You fail, and I'll introduce you to Russia." He pronounced it *Ruu-shee-a*, before pulling away from the curb with his back tires spinning.

I walked into my home with Jahliya in tow. We were greeted at the door by my mother, who immediately scooped up her granddaughter. "We gotta get you cleaned up honey. That bad man put his filthy hands on you." She walked to the kitchen with me close behind her. "Why are they messing with you again, Taurus? I thought that that white man and his daughter was out of our lives for good. I told you that nothin' positive comes from fuckin' with white girls."

She grabbed the first aid kit and began to stitch up Jahliya's neck, while I sent Princess text message after text message informing her that we had an emergency at home with our child. I waited for her immediate response but received none. I looked to see if she'd read the messages and saw that she hadn't.

Me: Hello? Princess?? Are you there??

I was beginning to worry about her.

I soaked my face in a sink full of ice cold water and held it under there for as long as I could. I was trying to get the swelling to go down and the bleeding to stop. My jaw felt fractured on my right side, but I was able to still open and close my mouth, which was a blessing.

"Momma, I gotta find that girl. That's all there is to it. Serge gave me a week, so I gotta week to do what I need to do to get her in front of him. It's the only chance we got at surviving this ordeal."

I sank my face back under water and allowed for the ice to numb my grill. It hurt so bad that I couldn't think straight.

I wanted to reach out to Hood Rich, but I knew that it would have been stupid of me. That wasn't how it went. When it was time for us to link up, he always got into contact with me.

I was scheduled to fly out tomorrow night to meet him back in Chicago anyway. Once I got there, I would tell him everything that took place and we'd hopefully come up with a plan to find Nastia together.

That night after my mother put Jahliya to bed, she knocked on my bedroom door, then she peeked her head in. "You up, baby?"

I was laying on my back missing Princess and trying to figure out how I was going to outsmart Serge.

On the big, smart screen television that hung on our bedroom wall was the Cleve-land Cavaliers game that I was watching on repeat. Sometimes just watching LeBron do his thing calmed me down. I don't know why, but in my mind, I considered him the ultimate thinker.

"Nall, Momma, I'm awake. Every time I try and close my eyes, I see the image of that Russian slicing into my daughter's neck with his knife. I wanna kill that punk. I'm tired of going through this stuff with him."

She sauntered into the room and slid in the bed beside me, laying her head on my chest and placing her thick thigh across my waist. Her little gown rose showing off the bottoms of her ass and even with me being in a state of panic, it did somethin' to me.

"What's on yo mind, Momma?" I asked, placing my hand on her ass and just keeping it there.

She moaned and rose her thigh a little higher on my waist, causin' her gown to rise even more, showing me that she wasn't wearing panties.

"Baby, I think it'll be smart if I get Jahliya out of this house and take her back to Jackson with me until you figure things out. I want us to fly out first thing in the morning. I'll hit up Princess and let her know what's what. But..." She ran her hand up and down my stomach muscles, then she slid it into my boxers grabbing ahold of my dick.

Damn, a nigga knew that this shit between us had to stop. But, I couldn't help it. This woman right here man. "But what, Momma?" I asked already knowing what was good. I needed somethin' to take my mind off what I was faced with and on some real shit I needed my mother anyway.

She purred, then she pulled my piece out of my boxers, leaned down and kissed the head. "I need some of you before I go. It's been a while and I just need my baby. Is that okay?" she asked, sucking me into her mouth and going right to work while I rubbed all over that big ass booty.

"Yeah, it's good. Come on and get up here. We ain't got time for all of that. I need you to clear my mind before I jump on this plane with Hood Rich and get on bitness. I need you right now, Momma. So, get up here and do yo thing," I said, watching her straddle me with her gown around her waist.

She turned all the way around until her ass was in my face and pulled my boxers off my legs, then she leaned her head back down and sucked my pipe into her mouth in a 69 position. I looked up and saw the way her pussy lips were puffed up and it made my dick two times harder.

I grabbed her ass and pulled her down to my mouth, sucking on her sex lips and licking all over them, tasting her after not doing so for what seemed like years, though it had only been about seven months and some change.

"Oooo-baby. That feel so good. I been feenin' fo yo body, son. It feels so good." She spread her thighs wider and really bussed her cat open for me to attack and I didn't waste no time. I could smell her inner essence. Her asshole was right on my nose, I looked up at it and continued to slurp her kitty while she moaned all around my piece, spearing her head into my lap.

I rubbed all over that big booty. It felt soft and hot. Forbidden and lovely. It made me shudder from excitement and the pain in my jaw went right away and was replaced by a pain in my penis. I could hear her slurping and sucking me with tight lips. Her moaning got louder the nastier I got between her legs. By this time, I was slurping and sucking and going crazy eating her cat, loving every minute of it until she came all in my face, humping back into my mouth.

She sucked me harder and harder, tugging on my penis with her lips, her tongue went back and forth across the head, driving me insane while thoughts of what Serge had done to me and Jahliya tried to force their way into my mind. I tried to focus on what she was doing and not see his bitch ass face. Had to enjoy the moment with her because they were so few and far between.

She tugged and tugged, then she licked up and down my dick, playing with it, getting real nasty.

"Taurus. Taurus. I want you to fuck momma from the back, baby. I need you to fuck me as hard as you can, so I can go back to Jackson with a smile on my face. Can you do that for mommy, baby? Huh? My body needs it so bad." She sounded out of breath. I slid from under her, got to my knees and flipped her to her stomach, then I pulled her up so that she was on all fours with her long curly hair all over her face. She looked so sexy like that to me. "Yes. Treat me, baby. Do momma good. I need you tonight, son."

I smacked her on her thick ass cheeks, then I leaned down and kissed them, sucking on the globes, running my tongue up and down her crease from the back. Her pussy was oozing, dripping out of her and running down her thighs.

I squeezed her pussy lips together and watched the juice come over my fingers. Her cat was a little hairy, the hairs curled up because of her inner essence. I sucked as much of her juices from her lips as I could before she got to hollering at me.

"Fuck me now, Taurus! I can't take it no more! I need you to hurt my cat, baby. Hurry up!" She laid her face on the bed, reached behind herself and spread her cheeks making her pussy open up.

I put my head on her hole, grabbed a handful of her hair and slammed forward, impaling my pipe deep into her body once again, feeling that forbidden electricity shoot all throughout me until I was shaking like crazy.

"Uhhhh! Yes, son! Yes, baby! Now go! Fuck momma hard!" She bounced back into my lap again and again. "Uh. Uh. Uh. Uh. Yes. Yes. Yes. Son. Oooo, my baby! Oooo, my baby fucking me so good. I need you. I need you, Taurus! Uhhh! Yes!" She continued to slam back into me with all her might.

Her soft ass was crashing into my stomach. Her long curly hair was all over her face. Her head against the mattress, slightly turned to the side, while her titties bounced up and down, rubbing against the sheets. The whole image made me tear that good pussy up I couldn't help it. There was an animal in me that only her pussy could tame.

"Uh! Uh! Momma! This thang so good. I love it. I love it, Momma!" I groaned, piping her down with all my might while she crashed back into me with her hand between her legs playing with her clitoris.

"Taurus! I'm cumming, baby! Hit it harder. Fuck momma harder! I'm cumming, son! I'm cumming! Ohhh here it comes!" She screamed, bouncing back into me, milking my pipe. At hearing that, my balls swelled up and I started to cum deep within her channel, smacking her on her thick ass cheeks and grabbing her left titty, pulling on the erect nipple.

As soon as she felt my pipe going off, she reached behind her and turned around, pulling him out and sucking him into her mouth. Her tight lips made me cum harder than I ever have before. Looking into her green eyes, I noticed her hair was wild as a lion in the jungle.

She pushed me back and climbed on top of me, reaching behind herself taking ahold of my piece and sitting down on it. “Just let me cum one more time, Taurus. You know momma greedy. I’m addicted to this big thang, baby. It’s mine. I gave it to you,” she said, bouncing up and down like she was riding a horse. “Uh! Uh! Uh! Uh! Yes! Yes! Yes! This my baby! Mines. You’re mine, Taurus! You belong to me! Yes! Yes! Yes! Do you! Yes! Uhh-a! Hear me, baby! Huh! Ooo!” she moaned, riding me so fast that I could barely hold her hips. The headboard slammed into the wall again and again sounding like it was trying to go through it.

The springs on the bed squeaked loudly. It sounded like a bunch of people were in my room jumping up and down in the bed all at one time. I pulled her down and sucked all over her titties while I palmed that big ass. It didn’t stop her hips from working and fucking me like I owed her somethin’, she screamed. “I’m cumming again, baby. I’m cumming on yo dick again. It feels so good! It feels so good. Can’t nobody do me like my baby dooooo-a!” She hollered and started to shake uncontrollably.

We ended the night with her laying back while I sucked them perfect titties and rubbed all over her fat sex lips. I couldn’t believe how fine she really was and how much I was still so turned on by her. I don’t think I would ever be fully over my mother no matter who I wound up with and

I'm just keeping shit real. it was somethin' about that forbidden pussy that I just needed in my life. Once I crossed that line with her the first time, I had been addicted ever since.

The next morning, I got woke Jahliya up with kisses and packed her a suit case. Princess had still not returned my text messages or even read them yet. That caused me great concern. I didn't know what to do or think. I hit my mother with fifty gees and told her to keep my baby safe, before we tongued each other down and she rode away in her rental on her way to the airport.

About an hour after she left, Hood Rich's limo pulled up and I got in and headed to his private Jet.

Chapter 8

It was about twelve hours later, and I found myself inside of the Ada B. Wells holding a shotgun down some dark skinned niggaz' throat ready to pull the trigger if his father didn't tell Hood Rich where that fool, Meech, was.

I was tired of playing games, plus I was on the clock now. I wanted to get Hood Rich's mission done and over with, so we could focus on finding Nastia together.

He said he had a lead that we needed to follow but first we had to hit up the Ada B. Wells Projects in Chicago to get some information out of one of the kingpins that Meech had put on using Hood Rich's Rebirth heroin.

"I'm gon' ask you one last time and you betta answer me correct or my mans' gon' blow yo shortie's head off on my command. Where is Meech hiding out at?" He grabbed the older man by the dreads. He had a big bald spot in the middle of his head that made him look like a clown up top.

"I don't know what you talking about Hood Rich. I ain't seen that nigga, Meech, in weeks, man. Now why you fucking up my operation. I don't want no part of y'alls war." he struggled against the two body guards that were holding him roughly. Hood Rich walked over to the couch and picked up a big pillow that was used to sit on. He tossed it to me. "Blow his shit back. Now!"

Bloom!

I pulled the trigger, knocking his son's head from his shoulders. It splattered all over the older man's daughter lap. She got to screaming in her duct tape and shaking her head like crazy.

Hood Rich walked over to her and pulled out a .45. "This bitch finna be next if you don't tell me what the fuck I wanna know. Now I know this yo baby girl right here.

You don't wanna see her brains all over the carpet like yo son's, do you?" He asked grabbing a handful of her hair and yanking her head backwards. June Bug lowered his head. "You just kilt my muthafuckin son for no reason Hood Rich. You think I'ma let you get away with this shit?!" Her hollered and tried to stand up. The goon to the left of him smacked him so hard that he yelped in pain.

His bottom lip hung loosely from his mouth. I cocked the shotgun and walked over to the June Bug, putting the barrel right on his head.

"Nigga, fuck all this playin', time is money. Where the fuck Meech at?" I curled my lip under my mask and got ready to blow this nigga's shit back. I was tired of going through all this back and forth shit. It was either he was gon' tell us where Meech was or die holding his peace. Either way, I felt like both him and his daughter would be killed. It was just how Hood Rich got down.

June Bug trailed his eyes up to the barrel of the gun and started to shake with blood running from his chin to his neck. He coughed and then swallowed loudly. "Okay, okay. Man, I'll tell you everything but if I do, Hood Rich you gotta promise that you ain't gon' kill me nor my daughter. We ain't got shit to do with what you and Meech got going on. That's bitness over my head."

Hood Rich rubbed the side of June Bug's daughter's face with his .45, looking her in the eyes. "Tell me where Meech at June Bug, you on the clock, my nigga."

"Promise me, Hood Rich. You'll let us live," he whimpered.

Barn!

I hit him in the forehead with the handle of the shot gun, splitting his head. "Nigga, you ain't runnin' shit. Tell my nigga what's good. Now! Or else, muthafucka!" I put the barrel to his Adam's apple ready to knock his head off his shoulders.

But this time I was so irritated that I just wanted to go on a killin' spree. I was missing Princess like crazy. Hadn't heard from her since the day she pulled out of our drive way.

Blaze was blowing up my line and I hadn't had the chance to respond to her and I knew she was worried about me.

Serge sent me a text with the time I had left to find his daughter, and I was worried about my mother and my daughter's safety and well-being out in Jackson. I knew there was nowhere my family could hide, no matter where they were if Serge really wanted too he could find them and cause them great harm like he'd done so many times before.

I pressed the barrel so hard into June Bug's Adam's apple that it broke the skin. A faint trace of blood formed around it.

He swallowed again. "Okay, look, man. I'm supposed to meet up with Meech tonight over at the old glass factory on 145th. The meeting is set for eleven. I'm supposed to be getting a hunnit bricks of The Rebirth. If you'll trust me to make this transaction, you can bump heads with Meech right then. All I'm asking is that you let me, and my baby live. She's just a kid, man, and we already lost her brother," June Bug pleaded. He looked from me to Hood Rich.

Hood Rich rubbed his daughter's face, then his fingers through her weave. "I watched this lil' girl grow up, lil' homie. It's fucked up that her pops got her in this position. I'm still paying all the bills for her to be going to the private school that she is, and this is how you repay me June Bug? I think she better off without you, my nigga," he muffed her face, then he walked over and stood in front of June Bug. “When you meet Meech, do you wear a mask? And how many niggaz do he allow to come with you?” Hood Rich asked, moving me slightly out of the way so he could grab June Bug’s throat and put his pistol to his forehead. “And don’t lie to me either, nigga, because remember that I taught Meech everything he know. I turned that nigga into Big Meech, you get that?” he growled through clenched teeth.

June Bug tried to shake his head. “I ain’t gon’ lie. He let me bring three of my security with me and he be with the same amount of niggaz. I been copping from y’all for so long that it’s a trust factor there. He already knows what it is with me, Hood Rich.”

Hood Rich nodded his head, then he looked to the goon to the right of him. “A’ight then, check this out, Rambo, snatch his daughter up and take her in that room back there. I see how you been looking at her,” he snickered. “Pebo, you and lil’ homie coming with me tonight and we gon’ rollout with June Bug to meet up with Meech. Hopefully, I’ll be able to body this nigga tonight and we can go back to get-ting money.” He looked down to June Bug. “Nigga, if you lying to me that’s gon’ be the worst move you ever made. Now do you and Meech wear masks while y’all do-ing these transactions?”

He nodded. “You already know that’s how we get down out here in The Land. We don’t play them games here in the Chi. Who don’t handle bitness like that?” June Bug spat with a mouth full of blood.

Hood Rich smacked him with the pistol and started to choke him out with one hand. “Bitch ass nigga, is that a yes or a no?”

“Ack! Ack! Yes-ack!”

***

At 10:45 on the dot, we were in an all-blue Cadillac Escalade with Hood Rich behind the wheel, June Bug in the passenger's seat and me sitting directly behind him. Pebo was to the left of me.

We pulled into the old glass factory and the first thing I noted was that it was full of trash and big ass rats ran around all over the garbage, making loud screeching sounds that made my flesh crawl as soon as we stepped out of the truck.

It smelled like death all around me and about twenty yards from where we pulled our truck in at was a group of heroin addicts huddled up with a burning garbage can, sitting on their asses shooting up their dope, while others were laid on their backs nodding in and out of consciousness.

There was one stray dog that walked around sniffing the trash. He was so skinny that he looked like he was on the verge of death. I watched him walk past a group of rats and they all hissed at him in a threatening mode. He jumped backward and lowered his head, going in the opposite direction. Every now and then, looking behind him to make sure that they weren't following him to attack.

There were only three big lights in the warehouse and two of them were flickering off and on. The one that remained steady shone over the entrance where we'd driven in at. The stench of the place turned my stomach upside down.

Hood Rich stepped from the truck and opened the passenger's door for June Bug. "It's show time, fuck nigga. You betta hope that everything go smooth or my mans gon' introduce yo daughter to that grown shit. I don't get down like that, but he do. Live and you let live, am I right?" he snickered and pushed him forward.

"Man, he'll be here, Hood Rich. But once he gets here, you gotta let me do the talking or he gon' know that somethin' ain't right and that's gon' spoil everything." He nodded at the people over in the corner. "What's good with them?"

Hood Rich looked in their direction, then he waved them off. They just dope fiends. We gon' handle our bitness and then get the fuck out of the crib," he nodded at Pebo, cocked his assault rifle and slid under the truck.

I had two .9 millimeters on me already locked and loaded. If the shit hit the fan, I was ready to knock some meat out of either Meech's taco or anyone of his goons. I planned on leaving that warehouse with my life intact.

Hood Rich reached into the truck and handed June Bug a suitcase, then he held one in his own hand. I didn't know if he'd filled them up with money or not. All I knew was that he had plans on killing Meech on sight, so I didn't know how shit was going to play out, but I was gon' protect me at all costs.

About ten minutes later, I saw the headlights from two vehicles coming down the road way before two red Bentley's appeared at the same entrance way that we'd drove through.

The cars had tinted windows and looked like they were the new releases for 2020, fresh off the show room floor. They cruised into the warehouse and stopped right beside our truck, then the doors to both cars flipped upward and out stepped a man dressed in all-black fatigues, with black gloves, black boots and an AK47 in his hand.

After he stepped out, two other men stepped out also dressed in fatigues. They all had on black ski masks to mask their identities just as we had, though our ski masks were white.

June Bug cleared his throat and perked up, walking toward the first man that had gotten out of the Bentley, extending his hand. "Meech, what's good, my nigga?" he said as they shook hands and gave each other a half hug.

Meech nodded his head and looked over June Bug's shoulder. "Them the same niggaz you always bring?" he asked loud enough for us to hear him. June Bug nodded.

"You already know. I only trust a select few." Meech laughed and pulled his mask half way up his face.

Me personally I didn't understand what all the mask wearing shit was about anyway. There was no way I would do business with any nigga if I didn't know who he was. Identity was half the battle. If I didn't know who I was fucking with, then I could be set up on so many levels, just like Meech was at that point.

As soon as Meech raised his mask, June Bug raised his just enough for them to confirm each other's identities. Then I saw Hood Rich get ready to reach for his gun when Meech took a step back and upped his kay, put it to June Bug's face and pulled

the trigger.

Boom! Boom! Boom!

The fire from the barrel illuminated the warehouse. June Bug's face exploded before he fell to the ground in a puddle of blood. The next thing I knew, Meech had ten red beams on his forehead and face. I looked to my right and saw that all the heroin addicts from before were now heavily armed with assault rifles and running across the trash ridden warehouse toward us.

Meech held up his hands. "You don't wanna do this shit, Hood Rich. Bitch nigga, I know it's you under that mask."

Hood Rich took his mask off and threw it into the truck, upped a .45 and stormed over to Meech, swinging the pistol and cracking him along the side of the head so hard that he fell to one knee. "Punk ass nigga! Get yo bitch ass up!" he hollered.

Meech felt the blood corning out of his wound, he took the mask off his face and started to laugh just as the heroin addicts from before closed in and aimed their guns at him. The goons that had come with Meech stood still as if they were shocked and appalled. Meech got all the way to his feet, then Hood Rich grabbed him by the jacket and forced his .45 into his right eye. "Fuck nigga, what's yo last words so I can tell yo momma."

Meech laughed. "Nigga, you forget that I'm just as smart as you. You really think I'd come all the way out here and not know what was good?" He made a guttural call so loud that it hurt my ears. The next thing I knew there were green beams all over

Hood Rich's face and neck. I looked at my chest and saw that there was about ten on me. I looked up and saw real subtle movements from the top of the warehouse where the lights were corning from. It looked like we were out manned and out gunned. I felt my heart beats speed up. "Bitch nigga, let me the fuck go." Meech ordered and yanked away from Hood Rich, dusting himself off.

In one swift motion, he back handed Hood Rich so fast that he dropped his pistol and fell backward into me, causing me to stumble and lose my footing. I fell into a pile of trash and three rats ran over my chest to their escape.

Hood Rich bounced right back up and raised his gun, cocking the hammer. He scrunched his face and lowered his eyes into slits. "Nigga, you think it's a game a somethin'?"

Meech mugged him with hatred. "Pull the trigger, nigga. Go ahead. We'll both be two dead niggaz right here and right now." He shrugged his shoulders as all the shooters around us looked confused, not knowing what to do. Everybody had either a green beam on them or a red one. It was shaping up to be one huge massacre in which both sides would take a lot of casualties. Meech laughed. "Yeah, nigga, you living too good. You ain't ready to die like me, Hood Rich. You too used to having yo way in this life. You got too much to lose, but me, I ain't got shit to lose." He dropped his AK47 and upped a .40 Glock so fast that it blew my mind, then he pressed it to Hood Rich's nose. "I'll kill yo soft ass right now because you ain't 'bout that life like me, nigga. Tell that fool to hand me them suitcases, so I can get the fuck out of here or I'ma splash you." He looked over Hood Rich's shoulder at Pebo.

Hood Rich didn't have to say a word. Pebo stopped and picked up the suitcases that Hood Rich and June Bug had dropped in the mist of their commotions. He brought them over to Meech, turned to Hood Rich and smacked him with one hand and with the other, upped his assault rifle and pulled the trigger, giving him all chest blows.

Boom! Boom! Boom!

Hood Rich looked like he vibrated in place before he fell to the ground with smoke coming from his torso.

That's when all the gunfire started. I dropped down to the trash and rolled to my left as bullet after bullet was let off all over the warehouse. It sounded like the fourth of July on steroids.

Blocka! Blocka! Blocka! Boom! Boom! Boom! Whoom! Whoom! Whoom! Boo-wa! Boo-wa!

I got up and ran behind our truck and climbed in through the back door, getting all the way to the front of it, behind the wheel as more and more shots rang all over the place, even rattling the truck causing it to shake from side to side.

I started it up, looked through the windshield in time to see Meech scampering to one of the Bentley's, jumping into it and backing out of the warehouse as shots wet up his whip. He got out of the warehouse and continued to drive backward until his car disappeared up the road.

More and more shots sounded. I could see people getting hit and falling to the trash, as more ran around bussing their weapons until they were hit. It went on for what seemed like an eternity and the whole time I stayed ducked down in the truck.

I wanted to storm away like Meech had, but I wasn't about to leave Hood Rich like that. I couldn't leave behind my mans, so as soon as the gunfire subsided, I pulled the truck up next to his body and loaded him inside before stepping on the gas.

"Aw! Aw! That bitch ass nigga, Taurus! That bitch ass nigga… caught me slipping!" he hollered with tears in his eyes. "Aw fuck! This shit…fuckkk …hurt so much." He groaned, pulling out his phone fumbling with his GPS. "…this hospital right here," he pointed out on the GPS. "Take me to this one. I'm plugged here. We won't have to… to fuck with the law. Hurry up, lil' bruh. I owe you my life, nigga. Word is bond."

This whole night had my head fucked up because I thought Hood Rich knew what he was doing, but it appeared to me that Meech was the real boss and for us to bring him down, it was gon' take some intense thinking ahead.

I wound up getting Hood Rich over to Christ Hospital out on South Kenwood in Hyde park. Once there he told me to leave him, to fly back to Dallas until he got some more shit in order.

Chapter 9

It had been another two days and still there had been no word from Princess. I was more worried than I had ever been. It got so bad that I couldn't eat nor sleep. The house was empty back in Dallas because Jahliya was down in Jackson with my mother.

I was tempted to fly down there just to be with them, but I knew I didn't have the time nor space to do that. I had to find Nastia before it was too late. Three days had past which meant I was down to my last four.

On the night that I'd got back home from Chicago, I was missing Princess so bad and was so worried about her that I started chugging large portions of Hennessy, so much so that I wound up drinking until I passed out. I mean, I don't know how or when it happened. I just know that one minute I was turning up and the next I was falling out.

I didn't awake until early the next morning because the sun was shining so hard on my face that it was causing me to sweat like crazy. I opened my eyes, and everything seemed blurry, until they focused, and I saw that somebody was standing at the foot of my bed. I snapped my head and sat up and looked into the eyes of Nastia. She had a big smile on her face and ruby red lipstick.

"I heard you was looking for me, Taurus. Is that true?" she asked, walking around to the head of the bed. I bugged my eyes and could barely breathe from being in shock. I couldn't believe that she was in my house and standing over me like it was the most natural thing in the world. I jumped out of the bed and pulled her into my arms, hugging her tightly.

"Man, where have you been, girl? Yo old man on that bullshit again." I said, smelling her Fendi perfume.

She hugged me and took a step back, looking into my eyes with her big blue ones. “I know why he’s looking for me, Taurus, and it’s not why you think,” She said barely above a whisper.

I frowned. “He misses you, Nastia. He say you been missing for months now. He thinks I got somethin’ to do with you disappearing. This muhfucka talking about hurting my people again because of you and I can’t have that.”

She shook her head and sat on the bed as two big ass white dudes in suits came into the bedroom with guns in their hands and ear pieces. “You okay in here, Nastia? they asked, looking her over real closely.

She nodded. “Seal off the perimeter and give me an hour.” They nodded and left back out of the room, closing the door.

I didn’t even wanna ask because I already knew she was involved in some heavy shit. The less I knew the better. I slid alongside of her and put my arm around her shoulder.

“What’s the matter, Nastia?” The whole situation was blowing my mind. I didn’t know how she found me or how she knew I was looking for her.

I wanted to ask her so many questions but first I had to make sure she was okay. That was important to me.

She sighed. “Taurus, like I told you before. There is so much going on in this world that you know nothin’ about. Things that would blow your mind. I’m in way too deep and I’m so scared for what it means for me, but I can’t stop now. I have to finish what I’m doing. You’ll understand later.”

I didn’t like when she talked over my head. I didn’t like when she spoke about things I had no knowledge of. The last time we’d been together we were under attack by men that were trying to kill her and I. I still had nightmares from that

day, especially with the Alligators and all. "Okay, so baby you know I won't understand, but can you at least tell me why your old man wants you so badly?"

She looked up to me and blinked tears. "Taurus, do you remember the last time we were together, and I told you that I had somethin' to tell you, but I would tell you later?"

I nodded, "Yeah, right after I got my people back. You came on to the porch and said you had somethin' to tell me, but you never did, and I forgot to even ask you about it. So, what was it?"

She started to whimper, and her shoulders hunched inward. More tears fell down her face. "Well, I was pregnant, Taurus, and when my dad found out that it was by you, he went ballistic and beat our baby out of me." She sunk to the floor on her knees. "He beat me so bad, Taurus. He said that no daughter of his was going to have a baby by a nigger. That our child would ruin my family's blood line." At saying that last part, it was like all the waterworks took on a new life. She started to cry so loud that I sank down to my knees and wrapped my arms around her.

"Baby, it's okay. You got through it. You can't let your pops bring you down to your knees like this. Things will get better." I didn't know what to say to her because I could only imagine what she went through. Growing up, I'd watch my father beat both females in my house senseless daily. But neither had ever lost a child in the process.

Nastia continued to cry rocking back and forth in my arms. "He has to pay, Taurus. My father has to pay for everything that he's ever done wrong to me and my mother and there is so much that you just don't know. He's a sick man. The reason my mother is gone is all because of him.

Because of how bad he wanted me all to himself. I hate his guts so bad," she cried, grabbing on to my Polo shirt.

"Taurus! Taurus! You betta tell these crackers to get the fuck out of my face and let me in my house! Taurus! Where are you?" Princess said from the front of the crib.

I almost shot to my feet and fully neglected Nastia until my common sense kicked in and told me that would have been mean and ill advised. She tensed up against me as if she knew I was about to stand up and desert her. "Hold on, Nastia, we'll finish this conversation in one second. Let's get in there before your body guards kill Princess."

When we made it into the living room, Princess was mugging the shit out of one of the beefy security men.

"Don't think because I'm little that you about to keep me out of my own house. You gon' have to kill me first. Now move!" She reached and pushed him with all her might, but the big man barely moved an inch.

"Gustav, let her through. She's no threat to me," Nastia said, wiping tears away from her cheeks.

Gustav curled his upper lip and mugged Princess as he stepped to the side, eyeing her the whole time as if he wanted to be given the word to kill her.

Nastia was rolling with some hittas.

Princess looked him up and down, then she jumped at him. "Yeah, move yo big ass out the way before I drop you. Huge ass. Nigga gon' have the nerve to not even budge and I pushed his ass hard. Whew. Big ass white man." She shook her head and walked over to me, before looking over at Nastia. "Who the fuck is this bitch?" she asked, looking disgusted.

I lowered my head and shook it. "Chill, Princess. Now ain't the time for all that drama right now. This a friend of mine and she going through it. I'm trying my best to console her and get an understanding before she leaves."

She walked up on Nastia and started to sniff the air around her. "You been back there fucking my man? Huh?" She looked her up and down. "Pretty ass white girl like you. I know Taurus can't turn that pussy down." She turned to me. "You fucking her, Taurus? I mean you fuck everybody else."

Nastia held up a hand. "Me and Taurus are old friends and nothing more. You don't have anything to worry about. I just came to let him know that…"

Splash!

Gustav's head exploded, his brains spattered all over me and Nastia. Her other guard ran over to look down on him and there was a, *tink tink tink.* The window in my living room had three holes appear in the glass and by the time I looked back to the other guard, he was holding his neck with blood seepin' through his fingers.

"Arrrgh!" He fell backward, hitting the floor hard before his eyes rolled into the back of his head.

I tackled both Princess and Nastia to the ground and threw my body on top of theirs, as more shots came through the window, chopping our walls up.

"Get off me, Taurus. I gotta get out of here or they're going to kill me!" Nastia hollered and struggled to get up.

I continued to hold her down, thinking she was out of her mind. I felt if she would have run outside that for sure she would have gotten shot up. I didn't know who was shooting at us, but I knew they were aiming to kill.

More windows shattered, and the walls were being picked apart.

"Taurus, who the fuck is this shooting at us? What if my baby was in this house right now?" Princess screamed as more shots rang out.

Just then the door was kicked in with a loud boom! Then what seemed like twenty men ran into my home in all-black fatigues, heavily armed and wearing black ski masks.

They surrounded us with their weapons pointed at our upper bodies. One of them stepped forward and yanked Nastia up by the hair.

"Come on, bitch, you coming with me. There's a twenty-million-dollar bounty on yo head." I placed the voice right away and knew that without a shadow of a doubt it was Meech.

He yanked and carried her all the way out of the house while she kicked her legs and screamed. "Help me, Taurus! Please! Don't let him kill me!" were the last words I heard before she disappeared through the front door.

I was expecting for Meech to have his men air me and Princess out, but he didn't. They left behind him and had the nerve to slam the front door to my house.

Ten minutes later and Princess was still fuming. "Now you got us under the gun for a white bitch. I'm getting tired of this shit, Taurus. First this bull crap with Blaze, now this a whole other bitch I'm stressing myself out over. Where did she come from? Why was they shooting at her and us in the process?"

I sat with my head down, trying to explain everything to Princess but the more I talked it seemed like the madder she became until I got heated and switched up the conversation.

"Fuck that for right now. Where have you been at, Princess? Why you ain't at least text my phone?"

She went into the closet and threw a suitcase on the bed. "Taurus, I'm finna get the fuck out of this house. You got white people dead in the living room. A white bitch that just got kidnapped and you standing there like it's all normal, boy, bye." She started packing her things real fast. "We can talk about all that shit at another time. You really ain't got the right to be questioning nothin' I do, especially with this bitch being pregnant and all." She sucked her teeth and continued to pack.

I inhaled and got up. I had to get out of that room before I snatched her lil' ass up and spanked the shit out of her. She had me so heated and that coupled with' all of the other shit I had on my plate already.

***

It took me six hours to get rid of them bodies and get the house back in order as best I could. Princess had decided to stay put and help me. I wasn't expecting that after all the commotion between us. She was no doubt, my rida.

After it was all done, and their body parts were in black bags, I sat in my den and placed a call to Serge, so I could set up a meeting with him and try my best to explain my side of what took place with his daughter.

We had decided on a mutual location. He flew down to Dallas the next night and we met inside of the Hilton hotel on Cameron Drive. I sat across from him on the love seat while he paced back and forth in front of me.

Two of his bug Russian bodyguards stood in front of the door with scowls on their faces. They looked like big wrestlers. I didn't even know that Russians came that huge.

Princess demanded that I bring her along and after arguing with her for nearly an hour I folded. She sat on the couch to my right and her eyes went back and forth watching Serge as he appeared to be deep in thought.

She picked up the bottle of Champagne and sipped from it. "Look, man, we been sitting here for twenty minutes while you walk back and forth not saying a word. You need to tell us somethin' because we're already on edge in not knowing what's going on." She took another sip from the bottle, then held it between her legs.

Serge stopped in his tracks and gave her the look of death. "Excuse me, little girl? What did you say?" he asked, looking down on her.

"My lady right, Serge, what's the deal?" I added.

Princess sucked her teeth. 'I'm a grown ass woman, first of all. And I said you need to tell us somethin' because all we've been doing is watch you pace back and forth for the last twenty minutes. You could have did alla this muhfucking pacing back and forth and then called us to meet with you. Ain't nobody got time for that." She rolled her eyes and picked up the bottle getting ready to sip out of it.

Serge swung and knocked the bottle out of her hand, spilling some of the liquid all over her body in the process.

The bottle flew against the wall and shattered into a hundred plus pieces. He looked like he was getting ready to put his hands on Princess when I jumped up and in front of them with her behind me and him staring daggers into my face.

"Man, chill, Serge, this my baby right here. She means no harm. She just doesn't know how severe this situation is. But just know, I don't play about her, just like you don't play about Nastia." To the right of me, I noticed his bodyguards upping their weapons, looking like they were ready to gun me and Princess down. Serge held up a hand stopping them in their tracks.

He gave me a devilish grin with his upper lip curled and his eyes lowered into slits. "Then maybe you should teach her some manners and let her know who it is that the both of you are dealing with. Tell that bitch that I could kill her and not think about it seconds later." He hissed, looking deep into my eyes.

At hearing him call her a bitch and talk about killing her, it made me cringe. I mugged the shit out of him and clenched my jaw.

"Yeah, I hear you, Serge. I know you just fuming right now because of everything that's going on with Nastia." I couldn't help remembering that she'd told me that this punk muthafucka had beat my baby out of her.

I knew that without a shadow of a doubt that I was going to be the one to kill him one day for all his sins. I didn't know how I would accomplish it. I just knew that I would.

Princess pulled me by the shoulder and tried to move me out of Serge's face, but I resisted. "Nall, fuck that, Taurus. I don't care who this white man is. He ain't finna be smacking no bottle out of my hand, spilling champagne all over my Prada dress and then making it seem like we in the wrong. This ain't no muthafuckin' Roots." She tried her best to get around me, but I held her with all my might. "On some real shit, white man. I ain't scared of you. All you can do is kill me. Once I'm dead, I'm gone. But while I'm here you ain't gon' be treating me like no fucking slave. You gon' respect my mind or murder me. You bitch ass bully." She was trying with all her strength to get at his ss.

"Princess, chill, ma', its good. I know you heated, baby, but we in a no win position right now. Just let this shit slide for the moment. You feel me?"

I felt her resistance waiver a little bit. "Yeah, a'ight, Taurus. But I'm letting you know I ain't taking this shit laying down. Don't nobody put they hands on me like that. This is bullshit."

I turned around to see her eyes watering up. That broke my heart and told my soul that I had to be the one to kill this punk ass Russian.

Serge upped a German Ruger and stepped to the side, putting it to Princess' head. "You shut up or I'll blow your brains all over this fucking carpet, you black bitch. Shut the fuck up! I don't want to hear you say one more word for as long as you're here. Do you understand me? Don't say nothing, just nod that monkey head of yours. Do it."

She nodded, and I felt the tears slide down my cheeks. That was going to be the last draw. It was time for me to put my life on the line. There was no way that I was going to be able to let him talk to my princess like that. This was the mother of my children. My best friend. My right-hand man and the love of my life.

He looked over to me while he held the gun to Princess' head. "And you, Taurus, you're going to find my daughter and that nigger that has her and you only have a few days left to do it. The first thing you should have done when she contacted you was get in touch with me, but no, you didn't do that, which means that everything falls on your shoulders." He spit on the floor and gave me a sinister look, then he lowered the gun from Princess' head, walking across the room and pulling a laptop out of his brief case, sitting it on the table and opening it up. "You see, I know there are only a few people left on this earth that you care about, Taurus. One is right there," he said, pointing to Princess, "and the other two are right here." He turned on the screen and fixed the laptop, so I could see what was on it. Then he started to laugh like a maniac. "Don't you know there is nowhere that your people can hide from me. I'm obsessed with you,

Taurus, and I will be until you're no longer breathing. Look at them!" he hollered, with spit flying across the room.

Before I could clearly see the picture, Princess let out a loud scream and fell to her knees.

Chapter 10

Princess fell to her knees and shook her head from side to side, with tears running down her cheeks. She crawled across the floor and stopped in front of the laptop, getting ready to grab ahold of it to see it more clearly when Serge kicked her right in the chest with all his might. She flew backward and landed on her side, choking on her own spit.

That was it, before I could even think about the consequences, I upped my .45, ran up to him and wrapped my arm around his neck, pressing the barrel to his temple with all my strength, so much so that it caved into his skin, causing it to bleed.

"Tell yo men to drop their weapons and to lay on their stomachs right the fuck now, Serge! Tell 'em!" I hollered into his ear, trying to bust his ear drum.

He said something to them in Russian and they dropped to their stomachs after sliding their weapons across the floor.

"Okay, Taurus, now calm down. I didn't mean to hurt your little lady. She violated my orders."

I squeezed with all my strength, choking him. "Drop that fuckin' gun, you bitch ass muthafucka! Do it now!" I squeezed tighter, hearing him choke and the gun hit the floor. As soon as I heard that, I loosened my grip a little. "Where the fuck is my mother and daughter. I see you got them tied up somewhere. Where are they?" I pressed the gun into his temple with more force.

"Ah! stop it. Now you don't know what you're doing. Let me go, Taurus, and I'll forget about all of this."

I picked him up and slung him to the ground so hard that he bounced up off it. By this time Princess was getting to her feet, staggering just a little. She walked over to us and picked up the German Ruger that Serge had dropped, along with a pillow from the couch and tossed it to me. I caught it in the air, lowered it to Serge's knee along with my .45 and pulled the trigger.

Poof!

The bullet shot through the cushion of the pillow and into his knee cap.

"Awww! You motherfucker! Do you know what you just done?" Aww!" He hollered, reaching down and holding on to his bloody leg.

I was about to pop him again when Princess ran past me in a blur. I turned to look and see where she was going and watched her slump down to her knees with her gun raised.

Boom! Boom! Boom!

One bullet after the next slammed into Serge's bodyguards who had stood up with guns in their hands ready to protect their boss. I watched bullets eat up their faces and necks, before they fell to the carpet in a pool of their own blood.

"You bitch ass niggaz try to creep my daddy!" she hollered.

"Kill his bitch ass, Taurus! I know where our peoples at. That's the basement of our mother's house. I know her house like the back of my hand. Kill him and let's go. You know them people probably already been called," she frowned. "Let's go!"

I stood over Serge while he held his knee with blood oozing through his fingers. "Don't do this, Taurus. I just wanted my daughter back is all. It made me crazy. I'm sorry, you can understand, can't you?"

In that moment, I thought about all the ways Serge had crossed me and my family. I thought about Tremarion, and

Shaneeta. I thought about Tywain and his daughter and baby mother that Serge had killed. I thought about all the times he'd snatched us up and finally the killing of my unborn child. I bit into my bottom lip and let all ten in my .45 ride into his face and neck, over killing his bitch ass.

Boom! Boom! Boom!

His body leaped off the carpet again and again. Blood popped into the air and

the last sight of him that I saw was of his face mangled from the bullets.

Me and Princess shot out of that room and down the back fire escape, into the night.

We made it to Jackson fourteen hours later, damn near breaking every speed limit on the way to my mother's crib. When we got to her block, the first thing I noted was that there was a black Navigator parked in the front of it with tinted windows.

Me and Princess cut through a neighbor's gang way to get to the back of the house. In the alley behind my mother's crib was another back Navigator parked with tinted windows, looking identical to the one in front.

She crouched down beside me. "Damn, daddy. Its two of these muhfuckas. How we gon' hit both of they ass at one time without tipping they ass off? The last thing we need is for somethin' to happen to Jahliya or our mother," she whispered.

I nodded. "I know, baby. This shit crazy but we gotta figure it out. Them Russians don't play no games. Whenever they find out that Serge is dead, they gon' come for us real hard, so we gotta get momma and Jahliya out of there. Come on, let's see if the bathroom window is open." I ducked down and wound up back on the side of the neighbor's house, creeping low to the ground until I was standing right under my mother's bathroom window. Looking both ways to make sure that the coast was clear,

I stood up and slowly forced the window upward, it rose with little effort. "Hell yeah, baby. Its good. Now I just need you to give me a little boost."

Princess nodded and clasped her fingers, so I could step into them. As soon as she did, I placed my right retro Jordan shoe into her hands and boosted myself upward until I was half way into the house.

Once I got part way in, I wiggled myself all the way through and slowly fell on the floor, before getting up and taking out my .9 millimeter with the silencer that Tywain had gave me a while ago.

I put the gun in my waist, leaned back through the window and pulled Princess up and into it. Luckily, she only weighed a hunnit and eleven pounds, so she felt light as a feather. She fell through the window and got up from the floor with a twin version of my .9 millimeter. She walked up to me and stood on her tippy toes, kissing my lips.

"Look, I love you, daddy. You be careful because yo baby girl needs you. Never forget that," she kissed me one more time, then she went and ducked down by the bathroom door while I placed my hand around the knob, slowly turning it.

The door opened, and I stuck my head out. I could hear voices down the hall. A foreign language that I guessed was Russian. I stuck my head back in to nod at Princess and she returned my nod.

"A'ight, baby, here we go." I opened the door some more and stuck my head out, ready to enter the long hallway when I saw one of the big Russians making his way in our direction. I slowly closed the door back with my eyes big as paper plates.

"Holy fuck, baby, one of em' coming this way." I backed all the way up and raised my gun, ready to knock his head off when he came through the door.

"Un unh, baby, get yo ass over here," she said, pulling me and stepping into the tub, pulling the blue shower curtain around us. I looked down on her with my face scrunched.

The big Russian came into the bathroom and dropped his gun to the floor and almost broke his neck to get his pants down, farting all loud and shit. I could smell him right away and it made me gag. I hated the smell of a white dude's ass.

As soon as he got his pants down, he sat on the toilet and started to take a shit with his shirt off. He made some crazy ass faces and acted like he had a problem with flushing.

Princess pinched her nose and looked pissed off. She shook her head in anger and just when the big Russian started to wipe his huge, hairy ass, she pulled the curtain back and let loose with her .9 mill.

Poof! Poof! Poof!

His brains splashed against the wall, before he slumped to the floor with his ass in the air.

We stepped over him and into the hallway, crouching low to the floor with me in front headed toward the dining room. All the lights in the house were off with the exception of the lamp in the dining room. We sped up the pace a little, at the same time being cautious and on high alert. We traveled past the kitchen and then the living room and into the doorway of the dining room where I found a big Russian sitting on my mother's couch talking on his phone with a scowl on his face, as if he'd just been given some bad news. He sat all the way up and got ready to come to a stand when I ran up on him with no mercy unloading into his face.

Poof! Poof! Poof! Poof!

He fell backward and dropped his phone. His face full of holes.

I turned around and saw that Princess was already headed for the back door, opening it slowly, then entering the stairwell that led into the basement. I followed her close behind, looking all around for any signs of a threat to us and seeing none.

We got to the bottom of the landing and entered the basement and all I could hear was murmuring and moaning. I grabbed Princess' arm as if to ask if she was hearing what I was. She nodded and lowered her eyes, then she jumped up, and so did I. We ran into the basement all the way on business. There were two men that paced back and forth around my mother and Jahliya, as they sat in the middle of the floor tied up with rope and black duct tape. It was like me and Princess were on the same page because as I aimed at one she aimed and shot at the other.

Poof! Poof! Poof! Poof! Poof! Poof!

They flew against the wall caught off guard. The one that I was shooting up tried to grab for his weapon only to receive multiple shots to his cheeks. His head exploded before he fell on his side, shaking like an earthquake.

I ran over and untied my mother while Princess picked up Jahliya just as she was. I didn't think she would take the tape off her mouth because our daughter was screaming and that would have easily tipped our enemies off.

I grabbed our daughter from her and one by one we slipped out of the bathroom window and onto the ground.

Once there, we made our way along the side of the house and made our way back the same way we'd come.

Princess sat holding Jahliya in her arms, as I stood on the balcony of the hotel trying to get some fresh air. I knew for a fact that we were about to have the worst drama we'd ever had in our whole entire lives.

Serge was connected, and he represented a whole nation of monsters that I couldn't even begin to understand. I had to get my family out of the united states somehow, some way, and I had to do it fast, Blaze included because she was my family, as well, and so was the baby she was carrying.

I shook my head and looked out into the night, trying not to have an anxiety attack, but shit was really real.

My mother stepped onto the balcony and rubbed my back. "You saved my life again, Taurus. It seems like you're always doing that, which is why I never panic when I find myself in a bind. I know that you're always going to come and save me." She hugged me with her eyes closed. "I love you so much, baby."

I held my mother for a long time, not knowing if I'd always be able to come through for her and hoping that I would. My mother was my rock. I lived to protect her, and I knew that I would do anything for her with no hesitation, but now the stakes were so high that I was starting to doubt myself. I had to get her and my family out of the country.

The only person I knew that could help me with that was Hood Rich.

"Momma, I know you don't want to but I gotta get you out of the states for a while. These people that I'm up against are savages and I don't know what their capable of, but I know that they will not stop coming for me until I'm dead, and everybody that I love is gone, as well. So, you gotta go." I held her closer.

She shook her head and cried into my chest. "No, baby. I can't be without you. Aren't you coming with me, if even for a little while? I can't be away from you, Taurus, I just can't," she whimpered, holding me so tight that I could barely breathe.

Princess stepped on to the balcony with a sleeping Jahliya in her arms. "What's wrong with momma? Why she crying right now?"

My mother picked her head up. "Taurus saying we gotta leave the country and he won't tell me if he's going to be corning along too or if it's a basic good bye. I can't be away from him, Princess. He's the only child I have left and the only one on this earth that loves me the way that he does. I'd rather die than be away from my baby." She buried her head back into my chest, sobbing loudly.

Princess raised her left eye brow. "I ain't even gon' lie, she making me feel real jealous right now because shouldn't nobody be crying over my man but me. I get where she coming from but still. Uh, Deborah, why don't you take Jahliya back into the room, so I can talk to my man alone. Let me cry on him for a change, you feel me?" She handed her Jahliya, and we watched my mother walk into the room with her head down.

As soon as the door closed, Princess reached up and grabbed ahold of my chin. "Why you telling her shit before you even tell me. I'm yo number one, fuck all them mommy issues you dealing with." She pushed my chin backward in anger and I wanted to choke her as out, but then again that was my princess and it was just how she got down.

I lowered my head. "I gotta get y'all out of this country, Princess, before them Russians murder us all. I can't have the women of my family murdered on my account. I just bodied their boss of bosses. I can only imagine what's gon' happen when the word gets back to Moscow. I gotta have y'all in a safe place way before then," I exhaled loudly and looked up at the moon that shone bright in the midnight sky.

I didn't know what to do. I felt so lost and smothered with responsibilities.

Princess smirked. "Nigga, you ain't sending me nowhere. Wherever you gon' be, is where I'm gon' be. Them punk ass Russians don't scare me. What scares me is being in this life without you by my side. I don't love nothin' or nobody like I love you, Taurus, not even our child and I'm a mother. I should never be saying no shit like that but I am. You wanna know where I went for that lil' time that I disappeared from you? Huh?"

I nodded. "Yeah. That has been nagging at me a lil' bit."

She sighed. "I parked my car in front of your mother's old house in Memphis and I just stayed there for days on end. I sat there because it's where I met you, and it's where we began our journey together. I thank Jehovah for the day he allowed us to cross each other's paths, now I refuse to be separated from you under any circumstances. I'm just not going. I love you way too fucking much. You gon' have to kill me in order to leave me behind, word is bond." She pulled me to her and wrapped her arms around my neck, looking me in the eyes. "Do you still love me like you used to, Taurus? Like, am I still yo baby girl?"

I looked into her small, pretty face and frowned. "Baby, I love you ten times more than I did before and you will always be my little baby girl. I'm yo daddy and that will never change." She shivered and held me tighter.

"Tell me that again. It makes me feel so loopy. I haven't heard you say that in a long time, so say it again, daddy, please," she begged, humping into me a little bit.

I held her firmer, feeling her little body up against my big muscular one. She felt so fragile and so tiny in my arms, yet at the same time so sexy and enticing.

"I love you, Princess. You're my baby girl. I'm daddy. All of you belongs to me and that's how its gon' always be. You my muthafuckin' lil' girl. Get that through yo head."

She shivered uncontrollably and started to undo my pants. "You gotta fuck me real quick, daddy, for real. I need some of my daddy dick right now. I'm feenin' for it. And while you're fucking me, keep on telling me who I am to you. Please," she dropped down, taking my Gucci pants with her along with my boxers, then she stood and pulled up her Prada dress, yanking her panties to the side, before hopping on me. "Fuck me, daddy, and keep on telling me that I'm yo baby girl."

My dick slid past her sex lips and into her oven that was wet and slippery as hell. Her walls started to suck at me, pulling me in while I slammed her down on my meat with vigor. "This daddy pussy right here. You hear me, lil' girl. This pussy belongs to me and only me. You my baby girl! Mine!" I hollered through clenched teeth.

"Uh! Uh! Uh! Uh! Yes, daddy! I'm yo baby. I'm yo baby girl! Uh! Shit!" She screamed bouncing up and down on me faster and faster.

I was trying to kill that shit. Her pussy felt so good and tight. I had missed it so much. This was my little baby. My life right here. "I'm daddy. You love daddy dick? Tell me, Princess! I wanna hear it. Tell me!"

"I. I. I. Uhhh! Shit. I love my daddy dick! I love it. You my daddy! Uh! Uh! I love you daddy! So, so much!

Uhhhh!" she hollered, while I bounced her up and down loving that soupy pussy.

I sucked on her neck and became one with her body. With every stroke, I fell more in love with her and knew that I could never be away from her for a prolonged period of time. She was my rider; the love of my life and I couldn't deny that.

"Tell me daddy! Tell me that you'll never leave yo baby girl!" she whimpered with her face in my neck as she bounced up and down on pipe.

"I'll. I'll. I'll. Ugh shit! I'll never leave you, baby girl. Never! Never! I. I. I. Promise!" As I felt her starting to shake, I could no longer hold back my seed from shooting out of my body and into hers.

She screamed and dug her nails into my shoulders, tilting her head backward as my mother opened the door with a look of hunger written across her face.

After our fuck session, Princess sat on the edge of the bed with her head lowered, shaking it from side to side. "Why you gotta go and save this bitch, Taurus? Why we just can't let her ass get rid of that baby, so we can go on with our lives? I don't want this bitch hanging around you forever. I just want you all to myself. You're my daddy. Not hers."

I knelt beside her, as my mother rubbed Jahliya's back while she laid out on the bed. Occasionally her and I would make eye contact and she'd smile weakly, before diverting her eyes. I knew she was hurt and didn't really understand why I was sending her away, but there was nothing that I could do about her emotions. My job was to protect her at all costs and to make sure she was always placed in the best possible situation. I grabbed Princess' hand and kissed it.

"Baby, you already know I have to be a man and stand up to my responsibilities. I can't leave her nor my unborn child out in the street like that. You gotta let me be a man."

Princess shook her head. "You know what? As much as I wanna argue with you right now, about what I want you to do and how I need you to see things my way, I'm just gon' let this situation go, and I'll do whatever you need me to do. If you getting this broad out of the country, that's cool, but just know that I'm staying and I'm not leaving yo side."

I didn't know what to say to that at that time, so I just didn't say anything.

Chapter 11

It took me three full days to convince Princess to go and help Blaze get her things in order before I moved her, my mother and our daughter out of the country. I still wasn't quite sure where I would move them to, but I had to make sure they were somewhere safe.

We all arrived at Blaze's house down in Houston three days later. Blaze wanted to have a sit down to make sure everything was cool between all three of us before she agreed to travel outside of the states.

She said that she knew Princess had a bad temper and she didn't trust her, so before she prepared to do anything, she wanted to make sure there was no bad blood.

As soon as I stepped onto her porch, she flung open the door and ran into my arms. Laying her head on my chest and exhaling loudly.

"Damn, I missed you so much, Taurus. I'm so glad you're here." She looked over my shoulder back at our Range Rover that we'd rented in my mother's name. "Aww, you can tell them to come on in. I cooked and everything." She kissed me on the cheek and went into the house.

I looked over my shoulder at Princess and she gave me a look that said she wanted to murder Blaze in cold blood. Her eyes were low, and her forehead was scrunched up. She looked like a straight savage.

After we sat down and ate the meal, me, Princess and Blaze sat down in the living room while my mother and Jahliya went into Blaze's room upstairs and went to sleep or at least I assumed that's what they did.

Princess stood up and lit the fat blunt in her hand. "Look, Blaze, I'm gon' be woman about all of this because

I must, but you already know I don't want to share Taurus with nobody, that includes you and the baby that's growing inside of you. Now it ain't no disrespect, that's just me keeping it real." She took a strong pull off the blunt and blew the smoke to the ceiling before handing it to me.

Blaze rolled her eyes. "Princess, you ain't the one that got me pregnant, so I really don't care how you feel about me or my unborn child. The fact of the matter is that Taurus is my child's father. I love him just as much as you do, if not more, and I feel like it's his place to be a part of our lives. If it was up to me, I wouldn't share him either, but it's not, so I just gotta do what you don't do and that's stay in my lane and play my role." She flared her nostrils and looked up to me as if to say, what the fuck is wrong with this girl?

Princess wiped her mouth with her hand and bounced her feet on her toes, while she sat on the couch looking like she was ready to jump up and go ballistic. "Don't nobody love my man the way that I do, Blaze, let's get that shit clear right now," she said with her eyes wide.

Blaze laughed sarcastically. "How do you know how much somebody love somebody else? I swear, you be doing too much." She sucked her teeth and took a deep breath, closing her eyes and blowing it out slowly.

Princess smiled. "Okay, let's just calm down because as you can see we both don't like each other. I'm like this far from being on yo ass right now," she said, making the sign of an inch with the use of her thumb and forefinger.

Blaze snickered. "Yeah, and I'm like that far away from showing you that it ain't sweet. I stand on mine as a woman, trust and believe that."

Princess closed her eyes and got to bouncing her toes on the ground faster, blowing into her fist, trying to calm herself down. "Taurus, please tell us how we finna work this shit out before you be burying one of us tonight, word is bond."

"Yeah word is bond, like she said," mugging Princess with hatred. That had to be the straw that broke the camel's back because before I could even get up, Princess shot to her feet, and upped her .9 millimeter and got to pulling the trigger again and again.

With the gun in Blaze's face. "Punk ass bitch!"

Click! Click! Click!

She stopped and looked at the gun, then she started pulling the trigger again.

Click! Click! Click!

Before throwing it across the room. "Ahhhh!" She jumped on Blaze and wrapped her hands around her neck, squeezing with all her might. "Die, bitch! Die!"

Blaze struggled against her and they began to roll around on the floor, until I jumped up and broke them up, picking Princess up off Blaze because she had her down on the ground with her hands around her throat.

"Let me go, Taurus! Let me go! Let me kill that bitch. She don't respect me, and she never will!" She kicked her legs wildly.

"Respect you! How the fuck can I respect you when all you are is disrespectful to me and my unborn child? I've never done anything wrong to you, Princess. I was in love with Taurus way before you came into the picture and I'ma be in love with him way after you're gone," she said, holding her neck and backing away from the couch.

"Ahhh! You see what I'm saying, Taurus! That bitch keep on saying lil' shit to get to me. She knows what the fuck she doin'. I promise she do!" She tried to wiggle out of my grasp and jump down but I held her and carried her up the stairs and into one of the guest rooms, flinging her on to the bed.

"Calm yo ass down, Princess, damn! Now you already knew what it was gon' be before you got here. Had I not taken them bullets out yo gun when you fell asleep, you would have kilt that girl. Fuck! You blowing me right now." I turned my back on here and shook my head, trying to figure out how I was going to figure this situation out.

Princess bounced out of the bed and into my face. "So, it's my fault that I love yo ass so much? It's my fault that I don't want to share you with nobody? Huh, Taurus?" She covered her face with her hands and started to cry into them.

I turned around wrapped her into my arms. "Princess, baby look at me, please." I begged, but she was already breaking down too hard. She fell to her knees crying tears of pain and I fell with her, pulling her into my embrace. "Baby, please don't do this. Fuck! I can't handle this shit right now. I need you to be strong and to understand that I gotta stand up and handle my responsibilities. I'll never leave you or put anybody before you, Princess, ever, I promise."

Princess cried harder and held me stronger within her little arms. I could feel her shaking like never before. "I just love you so much, daddy. I want you all to myself. I don't want anybody to steal you away from me one day. I can't compete with that pretty bitch out there. I know I can't. And I'm so tired of trying to."

I was about to say something to soothe her soul when the door to the bedroom opened and Blaze stepped in with tears all over her cheeks.

"Princess, you steady saying that you can't compete with me when you don't see how much he really loves you.

No man has ever loved me the way that Taurus loves you and they never will, not even him," she sniffled and wiped away her tears, stepping further into the room. "I swear, I don't want your man, Princess. He's not mine, he's yours. I can't compete with his heart and that's exactly what you are to him, his heart. All I want is for him to be a father to my child and to treat me fairly. I won't try and step on your toes anymore. You have my word on that, as a woman." She looked into my eyes. "Taurus, anywhere you want me to go out of the country, I'll go, just tell me where and promise me that you won't forget about me and our child. I need to get as far away from you as possible for right now because the love I have for you is going to kill me and if it don't, she will."

"Blaze, I'm so sorry, man. I never meant to hurt you and I wish I could be there for you equally, but I love Princess so much. This my rock right here and I gotta do right by her in every way that I can."

She nodded with her tears running into her mouth. "I know, Taurus, and I forgive you. Just don't turn your back on me and our child. That's all I ask."

Princess got up and walked over to Blaze. And it blew my mind when they hugged each other for over five minutes straight.

Both were crying and not saying a word.

Afterward Princess broke the hug and continued to hold Blaze's hands. "I'm sorry for ever disrespecting you or for calling you out of your name 'cuz you never deserved any of that treatment. I should have been more woman than that. If it's one thing that this me-too movement is showing us, it's that us women need to stick together and protect one another. So, I'm sorry and in any way that I can support you during all of this, please just let me know and I got you, my sista."

Blaze hugged her tightly and looked deep into my eyes. "Yeah, and I got you, too, I promise I do."

That night, Hood Rich hit me up at four in the morning saying that it was time to rollout because he had the ups on Meech and we had to close that last chapter before our lives could move forward.

I got an understanding with the ladies and promised them I would be back in a few days and that when I got back, I'd know where Blaze, my mother and Jahliya would be going. They all agreed to support one another until I returned, and I left feeling optimistic.

Chapter 12

Hood Rich leaned down and tooted up a thick line of cocaine, then he pinched his nose as I sat across from him in his mansion outside of Chicago, Illinois. He had two Rottweilers sitting on each side of him and they kept giving me a look that said they didn't like me one bit. I kept my hand right by the handle of my .40 Glock. One wrong move and I was finna knock they doggy noodles out.

"Taurus, whenever you see me tooting this shit, that means that I'm stressed out and looking to make shit happen by any means, lil' homie." He leaned down and tooted up another line loudly, then he coughed, grabbed the bottle of Moet and drank from it, before wiping his mouth with the back of his hand. "This nigga, Meech, got me stressed, kid, but I already know what I gotta do. You see when it comes to the game, every nigga gotta a weakness and I know what his is. Its only right that I exploit that shit."

A thick ass Brazilian broad stepped into the den and sat a gold tray down in front of Hood Rich that had twelve thick lines of some pink tinged cocaine on it. As she bent over, he rubbed all over her big ass that was encased in some red boy shorts that were way too small for her. Her ass cheeks hung out of the bottom of them and wobbled while he got his feel. She closed her eyes and ran her tongue across her thick lips, moaning deep within her throat as his fingers slipped into her leg band.

He smiled, took his fingers out and put them to his nose first and then sucked his fingers. I watched her walk away with her nipples sticking through her small wife beater.

"So, what you wanna do, Hood Rich, because I'm down for whatever, but we gotta get on it because as soon as we finish this shit, I gotta get my ladies out of the country before Serge and his army come at me. If somethin' happen to anyone of my ladies', man, I'd never be able to live with myself."

Hood Rich tooted two more lines, then he ran the cocaine all over his gums, coughed again before drinking from the champagne.

"I got some connects down in Brazil that I'ma have your ladies under the protection of. I got a nice lil' thing going down there and even though Meech fucked off his slot with my people out that way, you didn't, so I'ma put you in. But Nastia is the key. We gotta get that white bitch back, that way she can keep bussing the moves in our underworld, Taurus. Fucking with her got me and Meech filthy rich. I think the reason he snatched her up is, so he can call the shots and make it seem like the word is actually coming from her because that lil' bitch is powerful. Her old man got a bunch of higher ups that hate his ass and only fuck with her, but on the flip side, he got a bunch that love him to death and that'll sacrifice their life for him any day. It's a fuckin' Rubik's cube." He leaned down and tooted up some more of the pink powder, snorting it hard and loudly.

"Hood Rich, I don't know what you talking about. You know that shit way over my head. All I care about right now is the safety and security of my people and standing on my word that I made to you about being beside you when you brought this fuck nigga to justice. I got you, big homie, all I ask is that we step on the gas and make shit happen like ASAP," I said, lighting a blunt and inhaling the smoke deep into my lungs.

That whole world that Hood Rich was talking about scared me a lil' bit because it was so complex, and I didn't understand it one bit. I was yet to master the game of the hood, where as he was an international drug Lord. I just wanted to make enough bread to make sure that the ladies in my life never needed for anything. I felt like they were on my back and it was my job to provide for all of them as long as I had breath in my body.

Hood Rich sipped from the bottle of champagne and nodded his head. "Ride out with me tonight, Taurus, and I promise you after we done doing what we finna do, all this lil' shit gon' come to an end. You got my word on that. You just gotta be on yo no mercy shit to get results. From here on out, leave yo conscious at the crib and buss moves with me on yo heartless shit. You feel me?"

I didn't have no other choice other than to feel him.

Less than four hours later, I watched Hood Rich pick Meech 16-year-old son up by his neck and flung him against the wall in Meech's mother's dining room, causing him to fall through it.

"Get yo punk ass up, lil nigga, I ain't through with you," Hood Rich, said snatching the boy out of the wall by his dreads and flinging him to the floor, straddling his waist. "Open yo mouth, you lil' bitch ass nigga. Open yo shit wide so I can stick this .44 in it," he teased, then stuffed it down his throat when the little boy opened his mouth.

Meech's two daughters were already on the floor tied up, next to his mother and his baby mother. I didn't know what Hood Rich had in mind, but I was gon' have a challenging time killing them females if that's what he needed me to do. I could kill the lil' dude because I felt like he could possibly grow up and become the new Meech and seek revenge for what me and Hood Rich was about to do, but I felt like the females were defenseless and ain't have shit to do with anything nor would they have ever been a threat, either right then or in the near future.

Hood Rich stuffed the gun further down the little boy's throat, causing him to gag and dry heave all over the barrel.

"I watched you come out of yo momma, lil' nigga. You supposed to be my god son, but this what yo daddy done reduced me to."

Boom!

He splattered the carpet with the boy's brains and stood looking down on him. "Fuck nigga, look just like his punk ass father." He walked over to Meech's mother put the barrel of his .44 to her forehead and pulled the trigger.

Boom!

Her body jumped from the floor and then it was still, blood formed in a big puddle all around her. I didn't know what the fuck this nigga was on, but it seemed to me that he'd lost his fucking mind. I didn't know what killing Meech's family was gonna do besides make him mad.

I was so confused and even thought about stopping him from smoking them females because I didn't understand his game plan. When he picked up one of Meech's daughters that couldn't have been more than fifteen, I stepped in front of him.

"Bruh, I get clapping at this nigga, but what's killing his family gon' do besides make that nigga go kamikaze? If you kill everybody he cares about, he ain't gon' have nothin' to lose. I say we use them as leverage. Smoke that nigga out and when he gets close enough, then we murk his bitch ass."

Hood Rich bumped me out of the way, slammed the girl against the wall and pulled the trigger twice in her face.

Boom! Boom!

She slumped to the carpet twisted, two big holes in her face that oozed blood. I'd jumped back and looked at this nigga like he was crazy. I noted that his eyes were bucked, and his chest heaved up and down repeatedly as if he'd just ran a mile.

He yanked up Meech's baby mother by her weave and at first, the hair came out of place and wound up in his hand. She fell back to the floor, screaming in her duct tape loudly, before he threw the hair and picked her back up by the neck, slamming her against the wall roughly, putting the gun to her forehead.

"I told you, lil' homie, I'm on my no mercy shit. Every muthafucka in this house gon' pay for Meech's sins, everybody except Haley, right there,." he pointed at the last daughter, who couldn't have been older that ten.

She was caramel skinned, real pretty with curly hair. Around her eyes were red from crying her little heart out.

"You see all these bitchez gon' die but not Haley because Haley is my daughter, ain't that right bitch?" he said those words to Meech's baby mother.

I wanted to step in once again to stop him from killing his baby mother, but I said fuck it, took a step back and let him do him.

"All you had to do was keep shit one hunnit, bitch. Keep tabs on that nigga and never let him put his hands on my daughter, but you couldn't even do that with yo selfish ass. Now look at you, fucking with that nigga done turned me into a monster and you caught in the middle."

She struggled against him and shook her head from side to side, hollering into her duct tape, screaming again and again.

Boom! Boom! Boom!

Her body jerked three times in the air, then she fell on top of Meech's mother's body. The air smelled like bowel and gunpowder. As soon as he picked up Haley, his goons stepped in and drug the bodies toward the back of the house.

Seconds later, I heard the sounds of a chainsaw going off.

We left the house ten minutes later. After Haley got dressed, Meech put her into the back seat of his Range Rover. I got behind the steering wheel, while he sat in the back with her and I headed toward the highway.

"Haley, you know I love you, right, baby? You know that I would never do nothin' to hurt my lil girl, right?"

I looked into the rearview mirror as she nodded, with snot running from her nose. Tears were all over her face and she was shaking like a leaf.

"I didn't know that you were my daddy. I thought Meech was my daddy, Hood Rich. I'm so scared."

I felt sorry for her. She'd just lost her mother, brother, sister, grandmother and now the only father she ever knew. That was a lot for a little girl to go through in a life time, I couldn't even fathom in the span of just thirty minutes.

"Well, I am your daddy and I love you. That's the reason why every time I came over, I always had so many gifts for you and I made sure you were straight over your brother and sister at all times. Me and your mother went way back, but that's a long story, for now I gotta get you to safety while I finish this bitness. Lil' Homie, get off on Cottage Grove so my mans can pick my baby up and take her to safety. After we drop her off, we finna take care of some other shit and put pressure on a few of Meech's traps."

I nodded my head and stepped on the gas. I was still trying to see where Hood Rich was going with things but once again, he was so deep into the game that I just had trust he knew what he was doing.

As soon as I got off the exit ramp on Cottage Grove and pulled through the lights, a red Porsche pulled up beside me and I saw that it was being driven by a real fine Spanish broad. She waved for me to pullover.

"That's her right there, bruh. Pullover up there right by that McDonald's and she'll take my baby where she supposed to be."

I did exactly what he said. As I pulled over car pulled up behind me and Hood Rich took Haley and loaded her into the backseat. He leaned in and kissed her on the forehead before shutting the door. He talked to the driver for a minute, before she drove the other way.

Hood Rich jogged back to the truck and immediately got on his phone texting like crazy. "I'm finna show you how we get down out here in the windy city, Taurus. I'ma show you why I'm a muthafuckin' street legend."

Chapter 13

We wound up at a warehouse where we were met by about thirty niggaz in all black fatigues, black boots and ski masks. Everywhere I looked they were loading up assault rifles and hand guns. There were about seven black vans already pulled into the warehouse, all of them had tinted windows and no license plates. Hood Rich threw me a Mach .90 then tossed me two extended clips.

"What size vest are you, Taurus? You look like you about my size, I'm a large," he said, leaning into a green crate that said United States National Guard on the side of it.

"A large is cool." Even though it was going to fit me kinda snug, I liked mine to fit like that because it was already real heavy. The more loose a vest ran the heavier and more uncomfortable it felt.

Hood Rich picked up a AR-15 and slammed a clip into the bottom of it, then he tested out the beam by tapping the trigger. "We finna tear this city up, Taurus. I heard you brought Memphis to their knees but you ain't never did the shit we about to do, watch this."

Ten minutes later, we pulled up to Rockwell Gardens, which was a span of project buildings on the west side of Chicago that Meech was flooding with The Rebirth.

The area was dominated by Vice Lords that were cold blooded killers and strictly about their paper. We got there at about one in the afternoon and was met with a parking lot full of hustlers that had gold rags across their faces. They looked grimey. Their eyes were glossy and soulless.

Hood Rich pulled his big, black Hummer into the parking lot and the crowd of niggaz parted mugging the Hummer like crazy as if to say the driver must have lost his mind. I was sitting in the passenger's seat with the Mach .90 on my lap and a red rag covering it. On my head was a ski mask, but it wasn't pulled down just yet.

I watched Hood Rich jump out of the truck and leave the door open, then he turned around and reached under the seat, putting somethin' in his pocket, not once but twice, then he walked into the crowd of niggaz. I could hear him plain as day.

"Word around town is that you niggaz out here is serving my dope and fucking with that fuck nigga, Meech. Muthafucka, I'm Hood Rich, and where I come from, niggaz honor my gangsta and pay dues." He curled his upper lip, as about ten more niggaz came out of the building with their hats broke to the left and with guns in their hands.

They piled in with the crowd and then some lil' swole ass nigga stepped forward with long French braids and a yellow rag around his neck. "Around here we don't give a fuck who Hood Rich is. We Vice Lords and that nigga, Meech, got us eating. Any nigga an enemy of Meech is an enemy of ours." As soon as he said that, it seemed that every nigga in that crowd upped a pistol or a shotgun and aimed it at Hood Rich. "So, which one are you friend or foe?" The lil' swole nigga asked with a smile on his face.

Hood Rich dug in his pockets and came out with two grenades and took the pins out with his teeth, holding the detonators.

The crowd jumped back and a few of them started to scatter, and that's when five of the black vans from Hood Rich's army entered the parking lot from the other end and jumped out on business, firing looking through their scopes.

Hood Rich ducked down and ran back to the Hummer after throwing the grenades all the way up in the air. He jumped in the Hummer and sped backwards, as the shots came in our direction.

Pop-pop-pop! Boom! Boom! Boom! Whooom!

Both grenades went off at one time as we exited the parking lot with me holding my head under the dashboard. I could hear people yelling and screaming as more and more shots rang out. He stepped on the gas as another one of his black vans rolled past us and drove into the parking lot. I looked over my shoulder to see the niggaz inside hop out and get right on bitness, unloading their assault rifles.

"That's what I'm talking about, Taurus. That nigga, Meech, must've forgot that I'm a muthafucking savage. I don't play about my paper and I don't play about my loyalty." He drove about ten blocks, then he stopped outside of the Henry Hornets projects that Meech had also taken over and flooded with The Rebirth.

There were already four black vans parked in the parking lot, with the side doors ajar. I could hear the steady popping sounds coming from inside of the buildings. Hood Rich sat there for a minute nodding his head before he pulled off and got back on to the highway.

Later that night, we watched the news reporters do their best job to try and make sense of what took place on the west side of Chicago. They were saying that it was a major gang war, fueled by the quest to obtain more drug turf. I couldn't do nothin' but shake my head because they were way off.

"Cost me fifty gees, Taurus. Fifty gees to get the police to give me that area while I did my thing. It's all about money. Every fucking thing in this life is all about money. Them cops don't give a fuck about you or me or the fact that all those lives were lost. All they care about is feeding their families at the end of the day and lining their pockets with blood money. It's the game, baby boy. This shit is sick and only the stronger survive." He leaned down and tooted a thick line of coke.

I was still confused as to what all of that would have solved.

Later that night, I Facetimed with Princess. I was missing her so bad and I needed to see my baby girl's face. Hood Rich let me hook up his 27-inch laptop, so I could really see her good. She came on with a smile on her face.

"I been missing you like crazy, daddy. I can't keep on going so many days without you. It's starting to drive me absolutely insane."

I nodded my head. "I miss you, too, baby. I been thinking about you every minute. I think I'm super crazy about you now because I'm starting to get more and more sick the longer I stay away from you. You already know how I am and you know that shit ain't never been in me. So, I don't know what you did to me but whatever it is, you got me going nuts, baby. I need you, word is bond." I was serious as a heart attack. I was missing my baby girl like crazy. I needed to be in her presence. I needed to curl up with her ass and just hold her while we watched a movie or something. The life was getting the better of me. I just wanted to chill and be away from it for a moment.

"Awww. Really, baby? Are you really missing me that much or are you just saying that to make me feel good? I mean, either way it works for me but I still just gotta know because I ain't never heard you sound all putty and shit," she smiled, and her pretty face was doing something to me.

Them juicy lips with the mole on the top one and the lil' light freckles all over her face. That shit was making me crave her. "Nall, boo, I'm serious. I miss you like crazy and I need you right now. I'm almost done over here and when I'm through, I want you, me and Jahliya to take a nice long vacation where we ain't gotta worry about no drama. I just want us to live, splurge a lil bit and be happy. I think I been slacking on spoiling yo ass, so I gotta step my game all the way up and blow a couple bags on you. What you think?"

She smiled. "Shid, you know yo baby girl is a straight gold digger. If you talking about blowing a few bags on me, you already know I'ma sit back and let you blow 'em, then yo baby girl gon' blow you," she flirted, sticking her finger into her mouth and sucking on it.

She had me feeling some type of way. "How is Jahliya doing and where is she?" I asked, trying to change the subject because Princess was riling me up.

The screen froze, and I had to stop and set our Face Time up all over again. She came right on with Jahliya in her arms. "Here she go. Say hi to daddy, baby. Say hi, baby. Say hi daddy." Princess took her hand and made her wave it at the screen.

"Hey, momma. Hey, baby. You missing me?" I asked, smiling at the screen.

Jahliya smiled and started to wave her hand on her own. "Daddy. I love you, Daddy." She tried to grab the phone out of Princess' hands and Princess sat her back on the bed.

"She good, baby. I miss you like crazy, too. I can't wait until you get back to me. This Blaze broad is getting on my nerves again because all she's been doing is crying and spending all this time with your mother. It's aggravating me because out of everybody shouldn't your mother be spending most of her time with me? I'm just saying?" she sighed. "I can't wait until we send they ass off somewhere.

Both of them in love with my man and I don't like that shit. I need they ass gone, word is bond. I need my daddy all to myself. You belong to me for life, Taurus, I hope you know that. Taurus. Do you?"

I smiled and gave her both dimples. "I know, boo, and I'm ready to make that shit official. Don't nobody do me like you do and can't nobody love me harder than you can. You're my everything, all I care about is making you happy and giving you the best of everything. I mean that."

Princess blinked tears and held her hand over her mouth. "I miss you so much, Taurus. Please get back to me. Yo baby girl needs you so much."

That night after our talk session ended, I found myself yearning for her worse than I had ever yearned for anybody in my whole entire life. Prior to this, I didn't even think that dudes could yearn for a female, but I was damn near sick over her and I needed to be with her so bad.

I don't know what time it was when I passed out in the guest room of Hood Rich's mansion, all I knew was that he woke me up about five hours later with a big smile on his face.

"Taurus, get up. I found that nigga, Meech, and we about to go and get him before he can figure out that we on his heels. That lil' noise we made yesterday got them niggaz in St. Louis nervous. They ain't trying to see no action like that. Them country boyz all about they money. And for the right price, any nigga can be found. That loyalty shit goes out the window.

Chapter 14

Later that afternoon, after the plane landed, I found myself in sunny St. Louis, in the passenger's seat of Hood Rich's Benz truck, with three of his goons in the back seat heavily armed.

I had a Mach .90 on my lap once again and praying that I didn't have to splash a bunch of country boyz out that way. I knew them niggaz in the Lou' got down and the last thing I wanted to do was be playin' with them hammerz on somebody else's turf.

I was hoping we find Meech, murk his ass and keep it moving, then by later that week, I could have my lil' women in South America tucked away until I could figure out our next plan of action.

We pulled into a real grimey area that looked like the worst slums of Chicago and Memphis. There was garbage all in the middle of the street, with about fifty niggaz walking up and down it with pistols in their hands like it was the most normal thing in the world.

On the sidewalks were prostitutes that looked so nasty, a muhfucka had to be nuts to try and fuck one of 'em and not think he wasn't gon' walk away with a disease. I shook my head as they ran up to our truck trying to save themselves. I mean, they ran into the middle of the street and blocked us off to make sure that we looked them over and the closer they got, the more I was able to see the needle marks on their arms and the bumps all over their mouths. They looked sick, like they were walking corpses.

Hood Rich kept his hand on the horn and continued to drive forward, forcing them to get out of the way. "Man, them hoez look nasty as hell. I don't know what these niggaz out here in the Lou' be on, but that ain't what's up."

We passed a sign that said Kinloch Row Houses. As soon as we did, it was like the block took a turn. Instead of plenty dope fiends and old nasty prostitutes walking up and down the sidewalks, it now switched to some thick ass broads that damn near broke their neck trying to see who was driving the Benz truck.

The females were in groups of fours. They were dressed in little skirts that were so short you could see most of their asses and stretch marks.

As the truck rode past them, they'd shake their ass to a beat that had to be in their head because I couldn't hear one anywhere else. They tried to flag us down, but Hood Rich kept on rolling.

"Now I can fuck with some of them. Them just yo average hood rats looking for a trick. One thing about them show-me state girls, they'll fuck you and cook you something to eat before they hit yo pockets. I don't know, before I leave I might save a few of they ass," he laughed, as one broad bent all the way over, pulled up her skirt to show that she wasn't wearing underwear, before she started to twerk, holding her knees. Her thick, yellow ass jiggled and looked good as hell, I couldn't even lie.

Across the street from them was about forty dudes mobbed up and standing in front of some buildings, mugging the shit out of our truck. Majority of them had their shirts off, heavily tatted. Their mouths, from what I could see, were full of gold. They had scowls on their faces and as we rode right past them, they started to up their guns one by one.

"Taurus, keep yo hand on that Mach, lil' bruh. These niggaz out here think it's sweet. A muhfucka act like they wanna run up to this truck, we gon' splash they ass and get the fuck up out of here. I'll meet my connect somewhere else."

I put my hand on the handle of the Mach and cocked it. I was hoping I ain't have to body nothin', but if I had too, I was gon' make them bullets count. Luckily, them particular niggaz wasn't on shit with us.

As we rolled through Kinloch Row Houses, it was more of the same. The hood looked gutter as hell. All around there were kids playing and chasing each other. I saw a few basketball courts off in the distance that were packed with bodies. Little girls jumped double dutch here and there and there were all types of females everywhere. Bad ones, popped ones, it was pussy galore.

We got to the end of a street and Hood Rich made a right and turned into a parking lot that had about fifty niggaz in it with their shirts off, and guns in their waist bands.

As the truck drove into the lot, they surrounded us and upped their guns, looking like they were ready to buss. So, I took the Mach, put my finger on the trigger and waited for Hood Rich to give me the order, though my patience was wearing thin.

"Fuck should I do, big homie?" I asked, getting anxious.

Hood Rich reached over and put his hand on top of mine. "Calm down, I got this. If you hear me say Windy City, start eating these niggaz' face away."

A dark-skinned dude with plenty muscles stepped up to the truck and knocked on the window with rings on every finger. Behind him were two young niggaz that had twelve gauges pointed directly at Hood Rich.

On my side of the truck, two dudes had pumps pointed at me as well and they were pointed at our hittas in the backseat. Had them niggaz started bussing, we wouldn't have been able to get off many shots before they murked us. I felt my stomach turn over a few times.

Hood Rich lowered the window and the two barrels from the guns slid into the window along with the dark-skinned dudes face.

"What it is, Durty', 'bout time you showed up. I wuz starting to thank you wuzn't coming or somethin'. Who deez niggaz you got in hurl with chu?" he asked with a real country drawl.

The nigga breath smelled like shit, though. It was probably all them diamonds he had inside of his gold. He sucked his teeth and mugged me.

"These my niggaz, my muthafuckin' hittas. I know you ain't think I was about to leave the Chi' without 'em." Hood Rich reached under his seat and placed a Mach .90 on his lap.

The dudes outside of the truck cocked their weapons.

Chick-chick.

The dark-skinned nigga sucked his teeth and smiled. "You real funny, homeboy. Muhfuckas told me that you ain't have it all. How many shots you think you'd get off be foe my niggaz bodied everybody in this truck?"

Hood Rich shrugged his shoulders. "Nigga, this ain't no pissing contest. I came to do bitness with you, Lo'key. Now tell me where we about to have this sit down at, so you can give me what I need, and I can get you yo paper. Time is money, my nigga."

Lo'key mugged Hood Rich for a long time, then he slammed his hand against the window sill and took a step back. "Pull this bitch in that parking spot up there and get out and follow me, Durty."

I felt all kinds of butterflies in my stomach following this nigga into a project building that had about twenty niggaz standing in the doorway of it. They looked me and Hood Rich up and down with hatred it seemed like, then had the nerve to have two metal detectors right inside of the door.

"Say, Durty, I don't know how you city slickers roll down there in Chicago but down here in the Lou', don't no nigga come into our buildings that ain't fam with toolies. That shit ain't happening, Durty, that's just how it is," Lo'key said, looking from Hood Rich to me.

He'd already stopped us from allowing our hittas to come in with us. They sat in the truck, looking stupid as hell. I had a real uneasy feeling about all these niggaz. Hood Rich pulled out two .44s and handed them to Lo'key.

"Taurus, give the homie yo hand pistols. We ain't come down here for no bullshit, it's all love and bitness," he said, looking Lo'key in his eyes.

Lo'key ran his tongue across his diamond encrusted gold teeth and sucked them loudly.

"Yeah, Taurus, what he said. I mean, we only doing honest bitness, right?" He had a smirk on his face that rubbed me the wrong way.

I ain't like this nigga or these slums called Kinloch. I felt like this nigga was up to somethin' and I felt that Hood Rich was way too trusting for me. I wondered what he had up his sleeve because I knew he was a thinker and more than likely, he was always a few moves ahead, so I was in a position as to where I just had to trust his leadership, even though I didn't feel too good about it.

I took the Glock .40 from the small of my back and handed it to Lo'key, looking him in his eyes trying to detect any ounce of snake and I saw so much that once again I felt uneasy.

He smiled and gave a crazy ass laugh. “A’ight, now y’all just walk through this metal detector and we all good.” He led the way going through the machine.

I watched it beep like crazy, flashing red and I couldn’t help but to feel like a damn fool. How was it that we were allowing this dude to walk through a metal detector with our guns, but we couldn’t have ‘em? We were out of town and I felt out of bounds but once again, I had to roll with Hood Rich and let him lead. So, after he walked through the metal detector, Hood Rich walked through it and I walked right behind him and into the building.

Lo’key curled his lip. “Now I want you niggaz to enter into my world. Welcome to Kinloch, baby,” he said, waving his hands through the air.

Behind us the metal detector kept on beeping like crazy because more and more of his goons continued to cross through it, until me and Hood Rich found ourselves surrounded in a circle of about thirty somethin’ dudes. Most of them had their shirts off with pistols on their hips and mugs on their faces.

As soon as we got into the hallway, I could smell the distinct odor of crack cocaine. It smelled like burnt plastic and sugar. As we made our way down the narrow hallway that had graffiti all over the walls, there were a few apartment doors that were slightly ajar and I was able to look inside of them and see a sea of dope addicts laying all over the floors inside smoking the pipe or with their backs up against the wall and their eyes closed, just shaking their heads from left to right. Lo’key walked up to a few of these doors and pushed them in.

I guessed to give us a better view. “You see, Hood Rich, these are my people. They eat from me and they depend on me for everything.” Looking further into the apartment, I could see a young nigga at a table with what looked like a half of kilo of dope and a big pile of money, with two body guards behind him with shot guns.

He broke off one piece of crack at a time and sold it to a fiend that was lined up to purchase it. The fiend took the dope and walked back into the living room where there were about fifteen other hypes and sat down with his back against the wall.

Two skinny, older female hypes crawled over to him and they began flirting with the man all the while undressing in front of him. They were so boney that they looked sick. There were some already having sex in the far corner and the room smelled like funk, dope and death. I had to pinch my nose.

Hood Rich shook his head. "What this shit got to do with the bitness me and you supposed to be handling? I ain't impressed. I'm from the Chi'. I see this type of shit in majority of my spots. Let's keep it moving." Hood Rich grunted and shook his head. "I know that muhfucka stank, though. Damn." He pinched his nose just like I was doing.

Lo'key laughed. 'How the fuck you gon' come to my city and tell me how to give you a tour of my properties and operations. I hear you supposed to be the trap house King of yo city, so I just wanted to show you how I get down in the Lou', baby. This trapping don't stop. And that smell is the smell of success. Inhale that funky shit and honor my enterprise." He laughed and pushed in about six more doors as we walked through the hall, all of them had the same things going on as the first door he'd pushed in. It was like that landing was strictly for crack cocaine and dope fiend orgies.

Now if I thought that floor smelled bad. Once we hit the stair well and traveled up three flights of stairs, and opened the door, I almost fainted. As soon as we got on that landing, I saw four skinny females laying on the floor naked. They were so skinny that their ribs looked like they were trying to escape their body through their skin. They laid on the floor, with their legs wide open, the smell of spoiled fish was heavy in the air, so much so that I became dizzy and wanted to hurl.

Lo'key laughed. "Step over these hoez, man, and welcome to The Rebirth!" he hollered and stepped over the four females that were out of their minds and far away into their own zones. They scratched themselves and scratched between their legs as roaches crawled all over them. They acted like they didn't even feel them because for as long as I was standing there, I never saw either one of them shake any of them off. That gave me the heebee geebees.

We stepped over them and entered a dim hallway that was filled with dope addicts scratching themselves and moaning as if they were in pain. Almost every door in the hallway was opened and as we walked down it, I saw at least twenty hypes in each one shooting up their product, having sex or shaking and scratching all over themselves. All of them were ass naked and the heat on that floor seemed to be turned all the way up.

I mean, it was sweltering. I could barely breathe as we stepped over one body after the next.

"That nigga, Meech, got us eating out here, Hood Rich. That Rebirth keep my fiends happy. You see this shit?" he asked, opening a few of the doors further.

As I looked into most of them, I saw niggaz sitting at tables with dope all over it, behind them were armed body guards that watched their backs while they served their customers. This was a trap house by every definition of the word. I imagined the police running up into the building I couldn't see the dealers getting away because there were fiends everywhere. We could barely make it through the halls without stepping on some of them.

"I make a hunnit thousand a day just off this floor alone and its three of them like that in this building. You mean to tell me that once you knock Meech's head off that you gon' be able to guarantee that my operations don't stop? That I'm gon' be able to fulfill my clients every need when it comes to The Rebirth? Huh?" he asked as we made it to the end of the hall and back to the stairwell on the other side.

I was so happy to get there because of the fresh air. I felt like I'd contracted somethin' just being on that floor. I felt sick as a dog. I had to get the fuck out of the Lou'.

Hood Rich grunted. "From here on out, I'm taking twenty-five percent from what you was paying Meech for The Rebirth. And on top of that, every month you get ten kilos per order for free, that's just on the house because I see how you trapping. Long as you keep this shit going, you'll never have to worry about eating. I got you. I can also put you down with some of that pink lemonade Peruvian flake. It's that shit that the bosses in Columbia snort. Fresh off the coco leaf and purified without chemical. That fish scale is old news. I wanna plug Kinloch with that top notch shit for half the price the rest of the world getting it. Fuck with me and get some real money, Lo'key, not these peanuts. You supposed to be a boss and be able to take all these niggaz on trips around the world to show them the love that they deserve. The world is bigger than Kinloch. Fucking with me, I'll have you cultured, nigga. Money make this planet spin round, trust me when I tell you that."

Lo'key looked him over closely, laughed and ascended the stairs with all of us following him. When he got to the very top of the flight, he turned around and put a hand up.

"A'ight, my niggaz, I gotta talk bitness with Durty and 'em, y'all stay on S' and make sure everythang is everythang. Hood Rich, you and Taurus follow me through these doors right here, Durty."

I made my way through his crowd of killas until I was standing behind Hood Rich. I could really smell no ass or funk outside of the door and I was thankful for that. I didn't know what was on the other side, but it couldn't have been any worse than where we'd just come from.

Lo'key twisted the knob and pushed it inward and we stepped into a gray carpeted hallway, that smelled like Frankincense. There were five dudes standing about ten feet from each other with their backs against the wall and shotguns in their hands that were leaning up against their shoulders. Just like their comrades, they had evil scowls on their faces and a mouth full of gold. As Lo'key walked past them, they nodded at him and mugged the fuck out of me and Hood Rich. We got to the top of the hall and stood outside of a wooded door before Lo'key stepped up to it and unlocked it, pushing it inward. I could not believe my eyes.

He had this apartment decked out with white carpe all around, a big smart television up against the wall, with a white pool table in the middle of the living room and to the left of it was a Jacuzzi. All the sofas were white leather and it smelled like frankincense inside. I had to laugh at that.

"Y'all gotta kick them J's off, then have a seat so we can get an understanding amongst ourselves," he said, kicking his shoes off as well.

Fifteen minutes later, we were sitting on the sofa, sipping Remy Martin, while him and Hood Rich chopped it up. I was missin' my ladies and hoping that everything was okay with them. While they talked, I sent Princess a text asking her if everything was good. She text me right back and told me that it was and that warmed my heart because I was still real worried about all of them.

"So, if all that shit you said back there is true, then I'ma fuck with you the long way. I gotta make sure that my people eating at all times, Hood Rich. For me, that's what it's all about. Far as taking them trips and all that shit, that comes in due time, but it ain't my focus right now. What's good with that hunnit gees for Meech's head?" he asked then turned up the bottle of Remy.

Hood Rich wiped his mouth with his fingers and smiled. "You got a laptop? We can do this shit right now." He scooted to the edge of the couch and looked around as if trying to locate one. In the background were the sounds of Money Bags Yo spitting out of the speakers. I found myself nodding my head. I fucked with the homie's music, tough.

Lo'key got up and went to the back of the apartment and came back with an all-white laptop, handing it to Hood Rich. "I ain't all hood, my nigga. I know that cash ain't everything. That money that last is put up in banks, inside stocks and bonds."

Hood Rich opened the lap top and got right on business, while I watched the fish swim around in the big aquarium, with the white rocks on the bottom. I saw a few white baby sharks that had me fascinated.

"As we agreed, I'm giving you fifty up front, and after I knock this nigga head off, I'ma wire yo next fifty and give you another ten for the hospitality. I see myself fucking with The Lou' on yo behalf. If all goes well I wanna take you about ten of yo closest niggaz down to Brazil with me in three weeks and show y'all what that high life be all about." He clicked on the key pad for a few seconds. "Give me yo Chase info?"

Lo'key leaned over his shoulder and got to typing away before giving the laptop back to Hood Rich, then Hood Rich started typing. "There it go, this cash will be made available for your use in twenty-four hours. Now tell me what's good."

I sat back and listened to Lo'key give Hood Rich the entire rundown.

Chapter 15

That same night, I learned that no matter how high a nigga got in the game, every man had a weakness. For Meech, it was his weakness of little girls. Sitting back listening to Lo'key give us the run down, blew my mind. I couldn't believe that a man could be so sick, but then again coming from the land of R. Kelly, I guessed anything was possible.

At two o'clock that morning, Lo'key drove us out to the rich folks' side of town and into a gated community. When we pulled up in front of a big red bricked, three story mansion, he got out of the car and slid his card into some machine that allowed for the gate to click open. When it did, he got back into the car, then he drove into the gate and up the long drive way, before parking right out front. We jumped out of the whip and put our backs up against the side of the mansion, while Lo'key went around the back toward the pool house.

"Y'all just chill, mane. I'll be back and when I do, I'll be opening the front doe. They say the homie ass knocked out, been fucking all night and down heavy on that lean and Rebirth. Should be a cake walk."

He jogged along the side of the house, while I cocked the Mach .90 and got ready to splash some shit.

Hood Rich leaned down close to my ear. "I'm finna cut this nigga up, Taurus, so that every nigga in the game know not to fuck with my squad. You never cross a nigga that's feeding you. You supposed to die giving them yo loyalty, Taurus." He cocked his Mach .90 as well and placed his back against the wall screwing in his silencer, just as I did the same.

Ten minutes later, Lo'key came creeping down the side with a bloody knife in his hand. "Fuck niggaz. That punk got the worst security in the world. I guess after hitting all that young ass, they had to sleep that shit off," he said, then he waved for us to follow him.

My senses were on high alert, as we jogged alongside of the mansion, stopping outside of the back patio door. Behind us was a pool that looked to be about ten meters long. The moon

light shined down upon it, causing it to flicker in the night.

Lo'key stepped into the patio door, followed by Hood Rich and then me. The first thing I saw was two guards sitting on the couch with their heads tilted backward and their throats sliced so deep that it looked like their heads were barely hanging on by a thick layer of skin. I didn't know why Lo'key had decided to go that far. Why he didn't simply let us in and leave, but I looked at it as two less people we'd have to kill that night, so I was fine with it.

We stepped out of that room and followed him up some stairs that went into a spiral. I held the Mach out in front of me, ready to splash anything that jumped out at me or even looked like an enemy. I wanted to get this night over with and get on with my life. I was sick of the whole Meech saga.

After this, my debt would be paid to Hood Rich and my life could officially begin for the better. I was missing my ladies like crazy, once again.

We made it to the top of the stairs and slowly crept down the long hallway that smelled like sexed pussy. The aroma was heavy in the air. I could tell they had been doing some serious fucking all night.

Lo'key kept on going down the hall and I was waiting for somebody to open one of those bedroom doors and getting to clapping at us. I already knew that Meech kept some killas with him at all time, so I wasn't expecting for it to be a cake walk like Lo'key was saying. I just knew better than that. But as we got to the end of the hall and he opened the bedroom door, he took a step back.

"Wahla, there go that bitch ass nigga."

My eyes got bucked as Hood Rich ran into the bedroom. I ran behind him and saw that Meech was laying on top of the bed with about ten girls all over him. They couldn't have been any older than eleven years old, at least I didn't think so.

The sheets were pulled down just enough to show that they were naked from the waist up. Meech had a frown on his face as he slept snoring loud as a muthafucka. It was crazy.

Hood Rich slid his mask down and I did the same. Then he ran and jumped on the bed and straddled Meech, slamming the Mach into his forehead so hard that it bussed it wide open.

"Get yo punk ass up, nigga, and face this justice!" he hollered, then he smacked him again.

Meech opened his eyes wide and started groaning loudly. His groaning caused the little girls to wake up. When they saw what was going on, they started to scatter from the bed, screaming at the top of their lungs. It was then that I was able to confirm that they were all naked and black. I felt sick to my stomach, none of them looked older than twelve. Hood Rich went to town on Meech, bashing his head in, while I upped my gun on the little girls and made them lie on their stomachs.

"Everybody, get down before I shoot. Get the fuck down, now!" I hollered though shooting them was the furthest thing from my mind. One by one they fell to the floor following my commands.

As soon as they were situated, I yanked the sheet from the bed and covered them up with it. Hood Rich pulled Meech out of the bed, straddled him once again and kept on beating him in the face with his fist.

"You turn coat ass nigga."

Bam! Bam! Bam!

He beat him again and again, while Meech struggled against him seeming too weak to get up and fight back. He must have been too high. I noticed there was heroin all over the lamp table and a bog two-liter bottle of pink Sprite that was three fourths gone on the floor. I knew he was fucked up.

Bam! Bam! Bam!

"Where the fuck is Nastia, nigga? Where you got that white bitch at? Huh?" Hood Rich growled through clenched teeth, smacking him across the face three times.

Meech's face was full of blood by this time. He was fucked up. His eyes rolled into the back of his head. "Come on, Hood Rich. Don't do this shit, bruh. I love you. Come on, man. It's me and you. Just us, baby. Arrrgh!" He hollered and that caused the girls to scream.

Hood Rich took the blade out of the small of his back and slammed it into Meech's shoulder five quick times, then he pulled it downward, ripping his muscles to shreds while Meech kicked at the air and Lo'key looked on with a smile on his face. "Where is she?"

Meech sounded like he was running a marathon. He twisted his head from right to left and hollered in pain. "Mello, got her. She at his club in the basement. I'm sorry, Hood Rich. This dope got me fucked up. It's The Rebirth, man. I should have never done this shit, I swear," he groaned.

Hood Rich looked over his shoulder at Lo'key. "I got another fifty bands if you help me get this white bitch from Mellow. Fifty gees and twenty birds of The Rebirth. I want her back as soon as possible. What's good?"

Lo'key grunted. "Seventy-five in cash and them birds and we on." Lo'key pulled out his phone, looking Hood Rich over closely.

Hood Rich took his knife out of Meech's shoulder and nodded his head. "Bet, my nigga, make that shit happen." Then he looked down on Meech, raised the knife before stabbing him again and again, while Meech jerked under him. The blade punctured his

face leaving massive holes. Hood Rich could be heard breathing hard as he murdered his former right-hand man in cold blood.

Back at the hotel, I had to take shower to get the smell of dope fiend off me. As the water sprayed into my face, I got to thinking about Blaze and wondering if I was doing her wrong. I mean, for as long as she had been a part of my life she had been nothing but the best possible woman that she could be to me, never causing me any heart ache or pain. I wanted to do right by her but at the same time, I knew Princess held my heart within the palms of her hands. I lowered my head and allowed for the hot water to bead against me. There were so many thoughts running through my head at one time that I could barely think straight.

I stepped out of the shower, dried off and wrapped a towel around me, picked up my phone and attempted to Face Time with Blaze.

I needed to hear her speak from her heart just to see where she was mentally. My conscious was getting the better of me and I couldn't help it for the life of me.

She appeared in the camera with a big smile across her makeup less pretty face. “Hey, Taurus, long time no see, baby, when are you coming back here? I miss you?” she asked, looking directly into the camera lens.

“I’m about a day away and then I’ll be down there to make sure that y’all are taken care of. I miss you a lot, too, baby. How is our child?”

She nodded. “So far so good. Have you figured out where we’ll be going for sure yet? I’m kind of anxious to know, that way I can put a picture in my head of the region.”

“I don’t wanna say it over the phone, baby, but yeah I got that all figured out. Everything should be good; don’t you worry about that. The reason I’m getting at you right now is because I need for you to let me know what’s really on your heart in regards to us? I need to know that I’m not doing you wrong or hurting you in any way because I’ve never meant to, Blaze, I swear. You are very special to me.”

She smiled weakly and shook her head. “I don’t know how to answer that question, Taurus, without screwing things up because the fact of the matter is that I really, really love you with all of my heart and I wish that you and I, along with our child, could run away from everybody and just never look back for any reason. It’s all that I’ve ever wanted when it came to being with you. I think about you every other minute and I wonder why you didn’t choose me. Is it because I used to be a stripper? Do you think I’m not wifey material or something? I mean, just be completely honest with me because the suspense is killing me?” She sniffled, and a tear slid from her left eye, before she wiped it away.

I closed my eyes and rubbed my temples. This love triangle was driving me nuts because I really cared about both her and Princess, but I loved Princess so much deeper because she appealed to every fiber of me, whereas Blaze was more of an escape away from everything that I was faced with or had to go through in the slums and inside of the game.

Princess was from the gutter, just like me. A true hood chick that had been through it all including a forbidden past, just like me. When I looked into Princess' eyes I saw a woman that I needed to protect but when I looked at Blaze, I saw a woman that could stand on her own two feet and make things happen for herself.

I saw strength and I didn't feel needed as much. I loved her with all of me, but I guessed that I needed Princess with everything that I was as a man. She was my baby girl and I couldn't explain things better than that.

"Blaze, I love you, ma, and I wish that things were different because if they were, I would have been with you and living happily ever after by now. You are a good woman and I will always try and do the best I can to be there for you on all levels, especially when it comes to our child."

"Taurus, I hear all of that, but the one thing I need to know is that if Princess wasn't in the picture, would it be you and I for the rest of our lives? That's all I need to know. Just be real with me."

I didn't hesitate. "If Princess wasn't in the picture, hell yeah, Blaze, I would be with you faithfully, living happily ever after for the rest of my life."

She blinked tears and wiped them away from her face. "Okay, well, at least that's good to know. I mean, nobody wants to come in second, but I'll take it." Just then I could hear Princess' voice in the background asking her what she was doing.

Blaze looked as if she blocked the camera feed with her body. "I'm talking to my mother, I'll be done soon." Then I heard the door close loudly. "I gotta go, Taurus, but I heard you loud and clear and I want you to know that I will never stop fighting for us. I love you, baby, and I always will."

The feed went black just as Hood Rich opened the bathroom door with two thick ass strippers under his arm. "Taurus, these lil' hoez finna introduce us to The Lou', baby. You gotta go down there with me because this too much ass for me to handle. Y'all bend over and show my nigga what's good," Hood Rich said, taking a step back so they could bend all the way over for us.

They were two brown skinned sistas and strapped to death. Hood Rich had them ass naked already. Their bodies looked marvelous, little titties up top and thick down low, just the way that I liked 'em.

They stood side by side and bent all the way over until they were touching their toes. Wiggling their thighs, so that their ass cheeks shook heavy on their frames. I watched the cheeks open just enough to show a hint of their bald brown pussies and as exciting as it looked, I felt nothing. I had too much shit on my brain. Hood Rich rubbed their asses and squeezed them.

"Taurus, you can pick either one of them. Whoever you don't want, I'ma punish, then when you done fuckin' the one you do want, I'ma punish her ass, too, Windy City style." He laughed and smacked them both on the ass. They yelped and started to twerk hard.

I shook my head. "Nah, I'm good, big homie. I'ma sit this one out. I gotta get my head together. Shit ain't right, nah' mean?" I said, sliding past them and out into the room.

Hood Rich looked over his shoulder at me and the strippers stood up with their titties bouncing on their frames. “A’ight then, lil’ bruh, you get yo self together however you need too. I’m finna fuck both of them in the ass with my Sears Tower. I’ll be back out there with you in a minute and do me a favor and call these hoez an Uber in like two hours. I should be done with ‘em, then.” He closed the door and I could hear one of the strippers’ yelp as he smacked one of them on their ass, I assumed.

Chapter 16

Whoom! The door to the manager's office flew off the hinges as I kicked it with all of might. As soon as it was kicked in, Hood Rich rushed past me with two .44 Desert Eagles in his hands rushing Mellow as he attempted to get up from behind the desk to make an escape. But before he could, Hood Rich was on his ass.

"Bitch ass nigga, don't move or word is bond I'm finna hit you with every slug I got in both of these bangers."

Mello threw his hands in the air. "Say, mane, I don't know what all this shit about, my nigga, but if it's about the money, you can have this shit. It ain't worth stanking over, know what I'm talking 'bout?" he said with a mouth full of gold.

I noticed he had a gold ring on each finger and that there was stacks of cash on top of his desk. Behind him and lower to the floor was a safe that was slightly ajar. I couldn't really see inside of it, but I imagined that he thought he was going to be adding that bundle that was across his desk back to it sooner or later, until we came and rained on his parade.

I cocked the shot gun and slammed it into his chest as two of Hood Rich's goons stepped into the room with their pistols out. I could hear the sounds of 2 Chainz banging out of the system in the club.

It appeared that everything on the other side of the wall was going off without a glitch. I figured we had about ten minutes to do everything that we needed to do with this punk.

"Nigga, this ain't about no muthafuckin' money! Where is the white girl and don't play no muthafuckin' games with me or I'ma blow yo shit back!" I pressed the barrel further into him.

He sucked his teeth loudly. "Check dis out, mane, I don't know what white bitch you talking 'bout. You got the wrong…"

Boom!

The bullet ripped into his shoulder and knocked a chunk of meat out of him. It flew out of his back and I cocked that shotgun again ready to fuck him over some more.

"Arrrgh! Arrrgh!" he hollered, holding his shoulder as blood pooled through his fingers and dripped on the carpet.

He sat down in his seat and leaned his head backward with tears coming out of his eyes. "Huh, uh, what the fuck, mane. Why you niggaz ain't holla at Meech? This shit ain't got nothin' to do with me! Fuck!" he closed his eyes and tried to apply pressure to his shoulder, but it was of no use, that blood was oozing out at a rapid pace.

Hood Rich reached across the desk and smacked him so hard with the pistol that he made him spit blood across the wall, knocking a pile of money off the desk in the process. "Answer the fuckin' question, nigga! Where that white bitch at? We ain't gon' ask you no more." He aimed his .44 right at his forehead.

"A'ight, mane, a'ight. I'll tell you everythang cause y'all ain't gotta be doing me like this. Meech told me to take that white bitch and put her up until he was ready to…"

Something told me to look to my right and boy was I glad that I did because as the wall moved slowly backward, I saw a long ass barrel come out of it and then the shooting started just as I yanked Hood Rich to the floor.

Boom! Boom! Boom!

Fire spit out of the barrel before the wall pulled all the way back and two dudes came out bussing rapidly. Hood Rich's goons stood toe to toe with them, returning fire.

Boom! Boom! Boom!

One was hit three times in the chest. He fell on top of my back. I could feel him shaking as his blood began to saturate me. More shots were fired and one of the dudes that had come through the wall was stood up and riddled with bullets. He flew backward and hollered before landing on his side.

Hood Rich's goon knelt and kept firing his gun. Mello's security tried to run back inside of the wall but tripped over his comrade that had already been shot. He fell face forward and Hood Rich's goon ran behind him lighting his ass up with multiple slugs.

I watched him empty the clip, then I turned around and helped his fallen homie to his feet.

"Fuck we gotta get him to a hospital, man. Y'all come on. Please. I can't lose my brother, Hood Rich." He groaned, looking over his shoulder at us.

I hopped and leaped over the desk, grabbing Mello by the neck. "Enough with the games, nigga." I pulled backward and punched him so hard in the chin that he buckled.

By the time he woke up, me and Hood Rich had him in the basement inside of one of Lo'key's duplex's out in Kinloch.

Hood put duct tape over his mouth and taped his hands and feet to the chair. After he was in place, I walked over to him and ripped the tape from his mouth and smacked the shit out of him, showing him the knife that I held in my right hand.

"You don't wanna tell us what's good, we got a way of getting that shit out of you, trust me, homeboy." I stepped closer to him, took the knife and slammed it into the bullet hole that I'd left in his shoulder with my shotgun. Stabbing him and twisting the blade, while I grinded it into him with all my might.

"Ahhh!" he tried to jump from the chair, kicking his legs that were tied together. He struggled so bad that he wound up falling on his side and coughing up blood. "Ack! Ack! Okay. She at my spot over on Loomis. It's a barbershop, she in the attic chained up. Two of my lil' niggaz watching over her. Just let me go, man, and I'll get her for you. I can't take this shit. I feel like I'm dying," he said through gasps of air.

Hood Rich shook his head. "Nall, I don't trust this fuck nigga. I feel like he got somethin' up his sleeve. Bitch nigga, you was hanging around with Meech, so I know you got that snake shit in you. How we know this ain't no set up?" Hood Rich asked, kneeling beside his bleeding body.

Mello closed his eyes as tears fell out of them. "Just give me a phone, I'll call them. Matter of fact, take the phone out of my pocket and I'll tell you the number to hit. Let me holler at my lil' niggaz and let them know I'm coming and to have her ready. Once you see I ain't on no bullshit, y'all go get her and just let me go. This bitch ain't got shit to do with me. I was doing Meech a favor," he started to shake, and I could tell that the blood lost was getting the best of him. It would only be a matter of time before he was dead.

Hood Rich put his Jordan on Mello's neck and held him to the ground while he dug in his pocket and pulled out his I-Phone. Once out he made him give up the number, he then put the phone to Mello's ear.

"You bet not try shit, nigga, or I'm bodying yo ass."

Lo'key smiled. "Damn I ain't know you Chicago niggaz got down like this. I thought y'all was just on some shoot 'em up bang bang shit out there, but now I see. This what's up," he nodded his head in fascination.

"Hello, Telly, what it do, Durty? Say I'm on my way to get that white bitness. Have that ready fo me and by the back doe. I'll be there in half an hour," he gasped and blinked tears. I didn't know what the dude was saying on the other end, but all Mello kept doing was squeezing his eyes together tightly. "A'ight, I'll see you in a minute."

"What's the address, nigga?" Hood Rich asked, and he gave it to him. As soon as he did Hood Rich stood over him with his .44 Desert Eagle with the hammer cocked back. "Later, fuck nigga."

But before he could pull the trigger, Lo'key bumped him out of the way upped his pistol and fired two shots at Mello's face.

Boom! Boom!

Knocking his noodles all over the basement floor.

"This my city, homeboy. Can't have you city slickers coming down here and leaving no trail of bodies. Especially not in Kinloch. That's my job." He sucked his teeth and smiled, flossing his gold and diamond teeth. "Now let's go get this white bitch y'all killing foe." He shook his head and laughed. That nigga still rubbed me the wrong way because he seemed like he was off his rocker.

But never the less, we got to the barber shop fifteen minutes later. Lo'key had a crew of his niggaz rollout with us. We pulled into the back alley and jumped out of the truck. Lo'key and his crew jumped out of their blue Tahoe and ran into the back of the shop and the next thing I knew, Lo'key kicked the door in and they forced their way inside.

Gunshots sounded shortly thereafter. I ran behind them and by the time I caught up, I was stepping over two bodies and smelling gun powder in the air. There was a stair case that led to a basement, I took it and followed it all the way downward until I saw Lo'key coming across the basement floor with Nastia draped over his shoulder.

"This ain't the only muhfucka he got down here, homie. It's like five lil' black girls down there tied up, too. What you want us to do with them?" he asked, setting Nastia on her feet and pushin' her to me. She still had duct tape on her mouth, screaming through it at the top of her lungs.

"This yo city, Lo'key. Whatever you wanna do with them is on you, homie. All yo bread already wired, plus you got that other bag coming before I bounce tonight. That's my word," Hood Rich said, taking the tape from Nastia's mouth.

I never found out what they wound up doing with those little girls, but I just hoped it was the right thing.

An hour later, I was holding Nastia in my arms while she told me how Meech had screwed her over.

"I trusted him, Hood Rich, and I trusted you. I didn't think you guys would take my kindness for weakness. I betrayed my whole country for the two of you and now look where I am? I'm going to have to face them and then it's going to be war coming from all sides." She lowered her head and shook it. I feel so used." She wrapped her arms around my neck and laid her head on my chest.

Hood Rich continued to type on his phone, then he stopped and put it in his pocket. "You should have known that once the Don placed a ten-million-dollar bounty on yo head that Meech was going to screw you over for those peanuts. It's in his nature to be a snake," he shook his head.

Nastia nodded. "Well, yeah, had he done his homework he would have known that Don Bertolli had placed fifty million on my head and the golden key into the United Kingdom. Now that I could have seen him betraying me for, but ten million just wasn't worth it." She took a deep breath and sighed loudly.

"Nastia your father is dead, too. I had to put an end to his bitch ass. He tried to kill my people again and I wasn't having that shit. I bodied him a few weeks back. I just wanted to let you know." I loosened my arms from around her and sat back a little bit.

She shrugged her shoulders. "That's just the least of my worries, Taurus. Had you not killed my father he was going to have me killed anyway. This is what I was trying to tell you before Meech kidnapped me. My father knows about the black Underworld of narcotics that I have funded using our family's money and leverage. The only way for him to be able to save face and maintain his power and influence throughout my country was for me to be killed by his own doing. Had he not arranged for my murder they would have destroyed his empire from the top down." She shook her head and stood up pacing the floor. "I'm in way too deep. I don't know what to do. And now Meech has arranged for two tons of heroin to be shipped to the old glass factory tomorrow, along with a hundred pounds of explosives. These things were approved because he used my leverage and once they touch down, I am going to be responsible for owing a lot of scary people some impossible favors, which is why I have to cancel the order."

Hood Rich took his phone back out after it buzzed, and he read the message across the screen.

"Nastia, I don't know who up there in that Communist world that want you dead so badly, but the fee on your head has been upped to two hundred million and the key to the United Kingdom's heroin enterprise." He raised an eye brow and continued to read the screen as more words came across it. "All they want is yo head, too."

"Huh?" Nastia walked over to him and tried to look over his shoulder and that's when Hood Rich dropped his phone, twisted himself and got behind her pulling a knife from his inside fatigue pocket, placing the blade to her neck and slicing with all his might, squirting blood across the room.

Nastia gurgled and tried to scream but was only able to emit a soft squeal as Hood Rich threw her to the carpet on to her stomach and sat on her back, pulling her head back by her blonde ponytail, slicing her throat again and again.

I was so taken off guard that I was frozen in place. By the time I thought about getting up, she was already dead. I jumped off the bed. "Hood Rich, what the fuck, bruh?"

He slammed her face into the carpet. "Nigga, that bitch was a dead woman walking. You know how many killas she had after her for that type of paper she was speaking on? Fuck that." He wiped his mouth with the back of his hand, as Nastia blood continued to drip off the blade. "Now I just got direct contact from the Don Ciarpaglini and for her head, he's giving me the ins to the United Kingdom and Russia, places that I was never able to do my thing in, and with that two tons of heroin that Meech ordered through her. I'm about to have you set Clover City on fire, along with Brazil. You wanted to be rich. You wanted to live like me and Meech, well I'm finna help you eat, Taurus.

I'm finna show you shit that you ain't never seen before, all on a kingpin's budget. Trust me, lil' homie." He looked down at Nastia, her eyes were wide open and unseeing, the blues starting to go dim. "First things first is we gon' snatch up that heroin, then we gon' get yo people out of the country, before me and you go on a short vacation to Dubai. After we chill for a few weeks, then it's right back to bitness chasing millions at a time. How that sound?" he asked, looking me over closely.

I didn't know what to think or say at that time. I was too worried about Nastia's body in the middle of the floor. I knew for a fact that her death was going to come with repercussions. Not only was she a white girl, but she was heavily plugged in ways that I could only imagine.

The life that Hood Rich painted sounded good if I didn't have common sense, but fortunately I had a whole lot of it.

"Hood Rich, you don't think we finna have to pay for killing this girl and her father? Nigga, they was connected. If they could get Donald Trump in the White House, what the fuck you think they can do to us? Just think about it."

Hood Rick looked down on her and curled his lip. "Nigga, with two hunnit million and the paper from them birds we gon' be able to buy security like the white house got. You fuck with me and fifty million of that is yours out the gate and a two hunnit of them bricks. Now I know that seem farfetched right now, but trust me that lil' money go fast, especially when you spread out the way you gon' be." He wiped his mouth again. "Taurus, it's time for you to be a boss, my nigga. All that trapping in the hood shit is cool for the average nigga with no drive outside of the ghetto, but for men like you and me, we forced to think big. Forced to make shit happen on a scale that other niggaz could never understand. We got them women on our backs and we gotta keep them living good and with security. Now I wanna see you eat. I wanna see you be that nigga that yo old man never could be. You are the true boss of yo blood line, just let me help you prove that shit."

I lowered my head and shook it. I couldn't lie, I wanted to be that boss that Hood Rich was talking about. I did have a lot of mouths to feed and the women in my corner needed me to make sure that they never had to go without. I thought about that that first fifty million would do and it got me excited.

I wanted to make sure that my ladies were beyond straight for as long as I was breathing. I was a hustler by birth, and born to be a boss, just like Hood Rich. I couldn't even stop myself from smiling as I tried to imagine what Princess would say when I told her that I had fifty million put up in the bank for us.

She'd probably have heart attack. Fuck, I was missing her lil' ass so much. I needed to be hugged up with my lil' woman on that vacation that Hood Rich was speaking on. I know that me and her together would fuck plenty Indian hoez out in Dubai. That shit was gon' be hot. I couldn't wait.

"You know what, Hood Rich, long as we get my family to safe ground with a bunch of security all around them, I'm game. Nigga, I'll hold you down in loyalty harder than that nigga Meech ever did. That's my word. Just always keep at the forefront of your brain that my ladies come first in my life. I'm out here grinding for them, I worry about me later." I extended my hand. "Loyalty, big bruh."

He dropped the knife and wiped the blood across his fatigue jacket before shaking my hand and hugging me with all his might. "Loyalty, lil' homie. I'm finna make you a major boss, that's on my daughter."

I sat in a daze the whole time while on Hood Rich's private jet on my way back to Houston to get my girls. Prior to getting on the plane Hood Rich had said that jet was officially mine, for me to conduct bitness however I saw fit and my first order was to get my women to Brazil, in a safe haven, where they would be heavily guarded until I could figure out where we'd go next.

I didn't know how Nastia's people were gonna come back blasting, but the common sense in me told me that me and Hood Rich would not get away scot free from our past sins against them. I felt sick at even thinking about that, but it was my reality.

Hood Rich had a red Benz truck waiting on me at the hangar.

I loaded into it and rolled out into sunny Houston with the a.c. blowing like crazy. I'd already told the ladies that I would be picking them up that afternoon and I was hoping that they would be ready when I got there. I wanted to get as far away from Texas as possible and onto our new lives.

When I pulled up into the driveway of Blaze's house, I parked the truck and blew the horn three times before opening the driver's door and getting out of it.

As soon as I slammed the door and put my pistol on my waistband, the front door to the house opened and my mother appeared with tears all over her face and blood all over her white Eves St. Laurent dress.

She fell to her knees on the porch, then she got back up staggering, running down the steps and falling again to her knees, crying loudly. "Taurus! Baby! Oh, my God!" She jumped up and ran to me, then she fell into my arms.

I was starting to freak out as the sun beamed down on my forehead heating up my body. "Momma, what's the matter? Where is all this blood coming from?" I asked, expecting the worst. I felt my heart pounding in my chest, making me light headed.

"Taurus! She killed her! She killed her baby! Oh, my God!"

To Be Continued…
Raised as a Goon 5
Coming Soon

Coming March of 2018

A Drug King and his Diamond 3/19

By Nicole Goosby

Bred by the Slums 3/25

By Ghost

Blood Stains of a Shotta 2 3/31

By Jamaica

Coming Soon from Lock Down Publications/Ca$h Presents

BOW DOWN TO MY GANGSTA

By **Ca$h**

TORN BETWEEN TWO

By **Coffee**

BLOOD STAINS OF A SHOTTA **II**

By **Jamaica**

WHEN THE STREETS CLAP BACK **II**

By **Jibril Williams**

STEADY MOBBIN

By **Marcellus Allen**

BLOOD OF A BOSS **V**

By **Askari**

BRIDE OF A HUSTLA **III**

By **Destiny Skai**

WHEN A GOOD GIRL GOES BAD **II**

By **Adrienne**

LOVE & CHASIN' PAPER **II**

By **Qay Crockett**

THE HEART OF A GANGSTA **III**

By **Jerry Jackson**

LOYAL TO THE GAME **IV**

By **T.J. & Jelissa**

A DOPEBOY'S PRAYER **II**

By **Eddie "Wolf" Lee**

IF LOVING YOU IS WRONG… **III**

By **Jelissa**

BLOODY COMMAS **III**

SKI MASK CARTEL II

By **T.J. Edwards**

BLAST FOR ME **II**

RAISED AS A GOON V

By **Ghost**

A DISTINGUISHED THUG STOLE MY HEART **III**

By **Meesha**

ADDICTIED TO THE DRAMA **II**

By **Jamila Mathis**

LIPSTICK KILLAH II

By **Mimi**

THE BOSSMAN'S DAUGHTERS 4

By **Aryanna**

Available Now

(CLICK TO PURCHASE)

RESTRAINING ORDER **I & II**

By **CA$H & Coffee**

LOVE KNOWS NO BOUNDARIES **I II & III**

By **Coffee**

RAISED AS A GOON I, II & III

By **Ghost**

LAY IT DOWN **I & II**

LAST OF A DYING BREED

By **Jamaica**

LOYAL TO THE GAME

LOYAL TO THE GAME II

LOYAL TO THE GAME III

By **TJ & Jelissa**

BLOODY COMMAS I & II

SKI MASK CARTEL

By **T.J. Edwards**

IF LOVING HIM IS WRONG...I & II

By **Jelissa**

WHEN THE STREETS CLAP BACK

By **Jibril Williams**

A DISTINGUISHED THUG STOLE MY HEART I & II

By **Meesha**

PUSH IT TO THE LIMIT

By **Bre' Hayes**

BLOOD OF A BOSS **I, II, III & IV**

By **Askari**

THE STREETS BLEED MURDER **I, II & III**

THE HEART OF A GANGSTA I & II

By **Jerry Jackson**

CUM FOR ME

CUM FOR ME 2

CUM FOR ME 3

An **LDP Erotica Collaboration**

BRIDE OF A HUSTLA **I & II**

THE FETTI GIRLS **I, II& III**

By **Destiny Skai**

WHEN A GOOD GIRL GOES BAD

By **Adrienne**

A GANGSTER'S REVENGE **I II III & IV**

THE BOSS MAN'S DAUGHTERS

THE BOSS MAN'S DAUGHTERS II

THE BOSSMAN'S DAUGHTERS III

A SAVAGE LOVE **I & II**

BAE BELONGS TO ME

A HUSTLER'S DECEIT I, II

By **Aryanna**

A KINGPIN'S AMBITON

A KINGPIN'S AMBITION **II**

I MURDER FOR THE DOUGH

By **Ambitious**

TRUE SAVAGE

TRUE SAVAGE II

TRUE SAVAGE **III**

By **Chris Green**

A DOPEBOY'S PRAYER

By **Eddie "Wolf" Lee**

WHAT ABOUT US **I & II**

NEVER LOVE AGAIN

THUG ADDICTION

By **Kim Kaye**

THE KING CARTEL **I, II & III**

By **Frank Gresham**

THESE NIGGAS AIN'T LOYAL **I, II & III**

By **Nikki Tee**

GANGSTA SHYT **I II &III**

By **CATO**

THE ULTIMATE BETRAYAL

By **Phoenix**

BOSS'N UP **I , II & III**

By **Royal Nicole**

I LOVE YOU TO DEATH

By Destiny J

I RIDE FOR MY HITTA

I STILL RIDE FOR MY HITTA

By **Misty Holt**

LOVE & CHASIN' PAPER

By **Qay Crockett**

TO DIE IN VAIN

By **ASAD**

BROOKLYN HUSTLAZ

Raised as a Goon 4

By **Boogsy Morina**

BROOKLYN ON LOCK I & II

By **Sonovia**

GANGSTA CITY

By **Teddy Duke**

BOOKS BY LDP'S CEO, CA$H

(CLICK TO PURCHASE)

TRUST IN NO MAN

TRUST IN NO MAN 2

TRUST IN NO MAN 3

BONDED BY BLOOD

SHORTY GOT A THUG

THUGS CRY

THUGS CRY 2

THUGS CRY 3

TRUST NO BITCH

TRUST NO BITCH 2

TRUST NO BITCH 3

TIL MY CASKET DROPS

RESTRAINING ORDER

RESTRAINING ORDER 2

IN LOVE WITH A CONVICT

Coming Soon

BONDED BY BLOOD 2

BOW DOWN TO MY GANGSTA